特出版事業有限公司
st Publishing Ltd.

Adventures in the Fairy Tale World

童話奇緣

Follow Kuso 英語童話
來一場穿越時空之旅

克莉斯汀‧愛佐◎著

獨一無二的英語童話故事體驗

透過 **46** 個故事單元，大幅提升 **「英語力」**、**「創意力」** 和 **「思考力」**

晉升英語高手 成為說 **英語故事高手**

● **「情境對話」** → **融入道地歐美影集語彙**
能輕鬆地聽懂歐美影集 & 流利地進行英語溝通

「慣用語句型」 → **收錄特色慣用語與句型**
能靈活地運用於英文寫作中 & 悠閒地閱讀英語輕鬆小品

「文化角」 → **精選各故事文化風貌**
由淺入深地了解故事背景，遨遊異國文化風情

「啟發式學習」 → **由KUSO童話激盪讀者創意與思考能力**

MP3

作者序

你是否曾經有股衝動，想為童話故事裡的主角創造不同的情節與結局呢？當白雪公主正要咬下第一口蘋果時，如果你正好在場，會怎麼幫她化解危機呢？一向熱愛童話故事的我，很高興能藉由撰寫本書，讓童話故事裡的角色，一個個躍於紙上，並以不同的面貌，演出一齣齣精采好戲。

撰寫本書的另一個初衷，則是經驗的傳承。在學習英文的過程中，自發性地大量閱讀英文書籍，意外地大大提升我的英文能力。於是很幸運地，在面對臺灣不同階段的大考時，英文這一科目總能不費力地準備（也僅此一科而已，笑）。赴美之前在臺教授英文的那幾年，也常以自身學習經驗，鼓勵學生從找一本「適合自己的程度且喜愛的英文（故事）書」開始練功！

因此，由衷希望，本書能成為你的第一本英文 page-turner。讓搞笑的人物，詼諧又帶點緊張的故事情節，使你愛不釋手，一頁接著一頁地讀下去，同時還能輕鬆愉快地學習英文，吸收不同的文化資訊。

最後，在此感謝我先生 Travis Etzel 不藏私地，以英語母語人士的角度，給本書許多正面批評與建議，並在無數焚膏繼晷趕稿的夜晚，陪伴在我身邊，一同校稿。同時，也感謝辛苦的編輯韋佑和協助本書完成的編輯們。

克莉斯汀・愛佐（Christine Etzel）
2015 年 9 月 於美國愛荷華

目 次

1
Part

Into the World of Wonderland

Once upon a time, in the suburbs of the Windy city lived a boy named Tim BeauDaring, who thought of himself as an ordinary boy. However, an adventure in a fairytale world would change his life forever.

It all began with a basket of cupcakes that Tim's mom asked him to bring to Mr. Wizard, the neighbor who was living in a mansion next to them. After that very first visit, Mr. Wizard and Tim became good friends. One of the places they liked to hang out together was the greenhouse located at one corner of Mr. Wizard's back yard. Tim loved to observe the growing of plants and flowers. Most of all, he was very curious about what Mr. Wizard called his "herb experiment station", where thousands of jars filled with interesting dried herbs and unknown powders were located on the shelves. One day, Tim noticed a very special jar filled with a colorful powder....

Scene 1

In the greenhouse

Tim — Mr. Wizard, what is inside this jar? It looks so colorful, just like a rainbow.

Wizard — That's right. The powder is called the "Essence of Rainbow."

Tim — What a beautiful name. (*He looks into the jar.*) I think I see numerous rainbows in the jar.

Wizard — This powder is made of many magical ingredients.

Tim — Magical ingredients? Are you pulling my leg?

Wizard — Nope, I think my cat is pulling at your leg with his paws. He wants your attention.

Tim — Hahaha. That's why I feel something fluffy rubbing my right leg. (*He looks down at the cat.*) Hi, Mickey! I will play with you later.

Wizard ▸ Tim, you're a natural. You can be a wizard!

Tim ▸ A wizard? Are you daydreaming about yourself being a real wizard again?

Wizard ▸ Hahaha. Believe it or not, I have never been wrong about someone's potential.

Tim ▸ Really? You're talking like a fantasy author living in his own little dream world.

Wizard ▸ Well, I've been away from the World of Wonderland for a long time now. But the art of practicing magic does require some imagination.

Tim ▸ Okay, if I really can be a wizard, then I should be a wizard in my favorite fairy tales and save the world!

Wizard ▸ I like your ambition. A great Wizard with a good heart always brings positive energy and hope to the world. *(He quietly mumbles to himself.) This is perhaps someone we need in the World of Wonderland soon.*

Tim ▸ Yeah, yeah. You're talking as if I was someone else now.

Wizard ▸ Oh, by the way, the 'Essence of Rainbow' is very powerful. It can take you anywhere you want to go, but cannot return you to your home.

Tim ▸ What if I want to come back to our world?

Wizard ▸ When the time comes you'll have to figure it out yourself.

Tim ▸ Very funny. Anyway, thanks for the gift. Perhaps my mom would like to sprinkle some on top of her next batch of cupcakes.

第一幕

走進魔幻世界

很久很久以前，風城的郊區住了一個叫做提姆·博德林（Tim BeauDaring）的男孩，他覺得自己只是個平凡無奇的男孩，不過，一場在童話故事世界的冒險即將從此改變他的人生。

故事是這樣開始的，提姆的媽媽請他帶一籃杯子蛋糕去給住在隔壁大莊園的鄰居，巫師先生。初次拜訪之後，提姆和巫師先生變成了好朋友。其中，他們最喜歡一起打發時間的地方就是位於巫師先生家後院一角落的溫室，提姆喜歡觀察植物和花的生長，他尤其對巫師先生稱之為「藥草實驗工作台」感到好奇，這工作台上放著數以千計的瓶瓶罐罐，罐裡裝滿有趣的乾藥草和不知名的粉末，有一天，提姆注意到一個非常特別的罐子，裡面充滿色彩繽紛的粉末…

第一場

在溫室

提姆 ▶ 巫師先生，這罐子裡是什麼？好多顏色，看起來就像彩虹。

巫師 ▶ 沒錯。這粉末就叫做「彩虹元素」。

提姆 ▶ 好美麗的名字。（他往罐子裡的粉末瞧）我想，我看到罐子裡有許多彩虹耶。

巫師 ▶ 這粉末是由魔法材料做成的。

提姆 ▶ 魔法材料？你在扯我的腿嗎？（暗指：你在開我玩笑嗎？）

巫師 ▶ 不是耶，我想是我的貓正在用牠的腳掌抓你的腳，牠想要引起你的注意。

提姆 ▶ 哈哈哈，難怪我感到右腳有毛絨絨的東西在磨蹭。（他低頭看著貓）嗨，米奇！我晚點再跟你玩。

巫師 ▶ 提姆，你有天賦，可以成為巫師唷！

提姆 ▶ 巫師先生？你又在做自己是個真巫師的白日夢了嗎？

巫師 ▶ 哈哈哈，信不信由你，我向來不會錯看一個人的潛力的。

提姆 ▶ 真的嗎？你現在說的話就像是個活在自己的小天地的奇幻作家。

巫師 ▶ 那個，我已經遠離魔幻世界好久了，不過，運用魔法這門藝術確實需要一些想像力。

提姆 ▶ 好吧，如果我真的能成為巫師，那麼我應該要成為我最喜歡的童話故事裡面的巫師，來拯救那世界。

巫師 ▶ 我喜歡你的野心。一個善良的偉大巫師總是可以為世界帶來正面能量與希望。
（他小聲地自言自語）他或許是魔幻世界很快就需要的人才。

提姆 ▶ 對啦，對啦，你說得好像我是另一個人似的。

巫師 ▶ 喔，對了，「彩虹元素魔法粉末」的魔法非常強大，可以帶你到任何想去的地方。不過，你要想辦法自己回來。

提姆 ▶ 萬一我想要回到我們的世界呢？

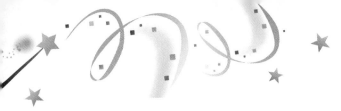

 巫師 ── 時間到了你自然會想出辦法的。

提姆 ── 一點也不好笑。總之，謝謝你的禮物，搞不好我媽媽可以 灑一些在她下批杯子蛋糕上。

Phrases & Sentence Patterns慣用語 & 句型

❶ What a + 單數可數名詞，用於讚嘆或感嘆，例如 "What a beautiful day！"

❷ be 動詞+ made of 由什麼組成，通常原料的原型已不見，如葡萄 釀成葡萄酒。

❸ Are you pulling my leg? 你在開我玩笑嗎？

❹ daydream about 做白日夢

❺ Believe it or not 信不信由你

❻ 以 do/does/did＋原形動詞，放在完整句子裡加強語氣，中文可 譯為「的確」「真的」，例如 "The dress does look good on you"。

❼ as if 彷彿，好像

❽ figure something out 想到（辦法），搞定

Cultural Note

Let's begin this Cultural Note section by asking ourselves the question, "What is culture?" Simply put, culture is what most people do or believe. But how do we define "most people"? The answer can be tricky, right? Culture can vary from one population to the next, one geographical region to another. For example, you may think that all Americans celebrate Christmas. However, people with the Jewish faith in the U.S. celebrate Hanukkah. If it is so difficult to define culture, what is the point of this section? Although the Cultural Note sections cannot cover everything (that would be a monumental task), the information can be useful when you need a topic to carry on a conversation. For instance, cultural subjects can be useful when you're trying to make friends with an English-native speaker or trying to break the ice with a foreigner at work. The most important thing to remember is to be confident and open-minded when learning a foreign language and other cultures. Now act like a wizard and make the Cultural Note sections magical for your English learning!

文化角落

　　在「文化角落」這一單元，先讓我們來想一個問題：「什麼是文化？」

　　簡單來說，文化代表多數人所做的或所相信的事。但是，如何定義「多數人」呢？答案可能非常難下，對吧？ 文化可能因不同族群，不同地理區域等差異而有所不同，舉例來說，你可能覺得所有美國人都在慶祝聖誕節，然而，信仰猶太教的美國人慶祝光明節（Hanukkah）。如果文化如此難定義，這一單元的用意又是什麼呢？雖然文化角落無法涵蓋全部主題（工程可能非常浩大），這單元所提供的資訊在你需要找話題延續一場對話時可能會派上用場，像是和英語母語人士交朋友時，或是在職場上要打破和外國客戶間的沈默時，最重要的是當你在學習外語和認識其他文化時，記得有自信並以敞開心胸接受不同想法。現在就像個巫師讓文化角落成為你學英文的魔法吧！

Scene 2   MP3 02

Back in Tim's bedroom, he takes some of the magical powder out of the jar and thinks about himself as a great wizard in the world. Then, the delicious smell of his mom's baking causes his thoughts to drift to the story of the Candy House. Suddenly, he sees a small tornado appear at a corner of his room. With astonishment, he grabs hold of the backpack sitting next to him tightly as he's carried away.

After flying around inside the tornado vortex for what seems like an hour, Tim finds himself falling into the bushes outside the Candy House. In the front yard, Tim sees The Witch of the Candy House and Hansel and Gretel peddling cookies and candies to passersby. The Giant of the Beanstalk approaches.

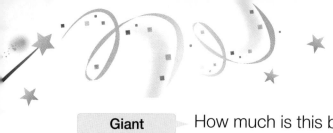

Giant How much is this bag of cookies?

Witch Buy two get two free!

Giant Oops! I forgot to bring my wallet. Can I trade you these golden eggs for a bag of cookies?

Witch Sure you can. But I thought your wife wanted you to watch your calorie consumption.

Giant Shhhh. Let's keep this just between us. Marriage can make people age quickly. I need some sweets to feel like I'm still young.

Witch Like a kid, huh? All right, this bag of Dwarf Cookies will make your dreams come true. Here you go!

The Seven Dwarfs suddenly jump out of the bushes and grab the bag of cookies from The Giant's hand.

Giant Hey, those are MY cookies!

Dwarf #1 Trust me. You don't want to eat these cookies.

Act One Scene 2

The Giant grabs the bag of cookies out of the Dwarf's hand forcibly and eats the entire bag all at once. Within minutes, he starts to shrink. He is now shorter than all of the Seven Dwarfs!

Dwarf #2 (*laughing widely*) Welcome aboard!

Tim (*talking to himself*) Oh boy! I guess Snow White will meet eight dwarfs now.

Wizard (*looking through his Crystal Ball*) This is going to be a fun training process for Tim. I can't wait to see what will happen next.

第二場

　　提姆回到自己的房間之後，從罐子裡拿出一些魔法粉，想著自己是世界上偉大的巫師。然後，他媽媽烤得香噴噴的烘培讓他的思緒飄到了糖果屋的故事。突然，他看到房間角落出現一個小小的龍捲風，驚訝之下，他緊緊抓住身旁的背包，隨之他就被龍捲風帶走了。

　　在龍捲風的旋渦裡飛了約莫一小時之後，提姆發現他自己掉落在糖果屋外面的草叢裡，他看到糖果屋的巫婆、漢賽爾（Hansel）和葛麗特（Gretel）在前院對著路過的人兜售餅乾與糖果。豌豆的巨人湊進攤位。

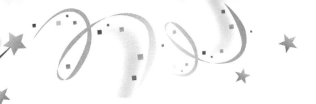

巨人 這一包餅乾多少錢呢？

巫婆 買二送二！

巨人 哎呀！我忘了帶錢包，我可以用這些金雞蛋跟你換一包餅乾嗎？

巫婆 當然可以，可是我以為你老婆要你注意卡路里的攝取。

巨人 噓～就當作是我們之間的秘密。婚姻讓人老得快啊，我需要一些甜食讓我覺得自己依舊年輕。

巫婆 想再像個孩子一樣嗎？好吧，這包小矮人餅乾可以讓你的夢想成真。拿去吧！
七個小矮人忽然從草叢裡蹦出來，並從巨人手中奪走那包餅乾。

巨人 嘿，那些是我的餅乾！

小矮人#1 相信我，你不會想吃這些餅乾的。
巨人硬是從小矮人手上拿走餅乾並立刻將整包餅乾吃掉。幾分鐘之內，他開始縮小，現在他的個頭比所有的小矮人還小。

小矮人#2 （狂笑）歡迎加入我們的行列。

提姆 （自言自語）天啊！我猜白雪公主這下會碰到 8 個小矮人了。

巫師 （透過他的水晶球看著發生的事）對提姆來說，這會是很有趣的受訓過程，等不及要看接下來會發生什麼事。

Phrases & Sentence Patterns 慣用語 & 句型

❶ With + one's 感覺／心情名詞，例如 "with amazement" 可譯為，令他感到驚訝的是…

❷ Buy two get two free 買二送二

❸ Sure you can 當然可以

❹ feel like 想

❺ Here you go. 拿去吧

❻ At once 立刻；馬上

❼ Within minutes 幾分鐘之內

❽ Welcome aboard 歡迎加入（行列、團隊等）；歡迎登機

Cultural Note

　　In the story of the Candy House, most people are familiar with the two children, Hansel and Gretel, who end up pushing the Witch into the oven to save themselves from being eaten. There was another sad part to the story. The family was very poor and didn't have enough food to support the children. Therefore, the children's mother persuaded her husband to take the children deep into the forest and leave them there. Hansel and Gretel's father doesn't want to abandon the children but eventually agrees to his wife's request. However, Hansel and Gretel leave a trail of shiny pebbles along the path and eventually follow them back home. Their father greets them with tears of joy. Interestingly, in the original story from the Brothers Grimm, their mother dies before their return home leaving the story unexplained. This might have been a moral lesson by the Brothers Grimm to remind parents to stay with their children no matter what.

文化角落

　　大部份的人都知道「糖果屋」這故事裡面的兩個小主角漢賽爾（Hansel）和葛麗特（Gretel），最後將巫婆推進烤爐裡才順利救了他們自己，沒有被吃掉。這故事其實還有比較令人難過的一部分，故事一開始他們家很窮，沒有足夠食物供給孩子們吃，因此，孩子的母親說服她先生帶著他們到森林深處，並將他們留在那裡，漢賽爾（Hansel）和葛麗特（Gretel）的父親不想要拋棄他們但最後還是同意他太太的請求，當他們最後終於回到家，他們的父親含著淚迎接，有趣的是，在最初版的格林童話故事裡，母親在他們返家之前已經去世，但故事中並未交代原因，格林兄弟可能是想透過故事做一點道德勸說，提醒父母無論如何都要待在孩子身邊。

Scene 3   MP3 03

| Giant | (*turning to the Witch*) Undo this magic immediately! |

| Witch | What is done is done. Hahaha! |

| Giant | You wicked little witch! |

| Witch | I am flattered. But I am not Elphaba, that green-faced witch. Hahaha. |

| Dwarf #3 | (*pating the Giant's back*) Wow, look at this! Now I can reach the Giant's back! |

| Dwarf #4 | It's okay, dude. You can be the eighth in our group. |

Tim is so fascinated with what's going on that he decides to exit the safety of the bushes and introduces himself to the group.

| Tim | Excuse me. Hi, I'm Tim BeauDaring. Can I take a picture of you? |

| Everyone | A picture? |

Tim Yes, a picture. Just get closer together and look at me here. Say 'cheese'. Awesome! This will be a great souvenir to show off.

Dwarf #5 (*talking to his fellow dwarfs*) What does 'take a picture' mean?
The dwarfs get into a heated debate.

Dwarf #6 We need to be cautious about saying cheese in front of a black box lest we will be sucked into the box. But, I think it's okay to eat cheese when someone takes our picture.

Dwarf #7 Oh, I have an idea! Let's try to say 'chop chop' together. Perhaps the little black box will be scared of us and will not eat us.

Dwarf #3 Why 'chop chop'?

Dwarf #7 We always use our axe to chop wood. This makes us sound strong!

The rest of the Dwarfs agree, so they start to practice saying 'chop chop' aloud. Meanwhile, the Witch makes Tim an offer.

| Witch | Hey, kiddo. Would you like to see inside the Candy House? (*Then she turns to the Giant.*) You too! Perhaps I can remember how to help you.
Tim decided to take the risk to check out the Candy House. |

| Dwarf #4 | Oh no, the boy has disappeared! |

As it's getting dark out and the Dark Forest can be dangerous, The Seven Dwarfs decide to return to their place.

第三場

| 巨人 | （轉向巫婆）立刻解除這魔法！ |

| 巫婆 | 木已成舟！哈哈哈！ |

| 巨人 | 你這壞心的巫婆！ |

| 巫婆 | 過獎了！不過我不是 Elphaba 那綠臉女巫，哈哈哈。 |

| 小矮人#3 | （拍拍巨人的肩膀）哇，你們看！我現在可以摸到巨人的背耶！ |

| 小矮人#4 | 老兄，沒關係啦！你可以加入我們當老八。
提姆對於這一切發生的事感到著迷，所以他決定離開安全 |

的草叢，向大家介紹自己。

提姆 不好意思，我是提姆・博德林（Tim BeauDaring）。你們可以讓我拍張照嗎？

所有的人 拍張照？

提姆 對，拍照。大家靠近一點並看我這裡，說「起司」。太讚了！這紀念品拿來炫耀超棒的。

小矮人#5 （對他其他小矮人伙伴說）「拍照」是什麼意思啊？
小矮人們陷入熱烈的辯論當中。

小矮人#6 我們在那個黑色盒子前說「起司」時需要謹慎一些，以免被吸進盒子裡，不過我覺得當人家替我們拍照時，吃起司應該沒關係。

小矮人#7 喔，我有個點子！我們齊聲試著說「砍砍砍」，或許這小黑盒會害怕而不敢吃掉我們。

小矮人#6 為什麼是「砍砍砍」？

小矮人#7 我們總是用斧頭在砍木頭，這聲音讓我們聽起來很強壯！
其他的小矮人都同意，所以他們開始練習發出很大聲的「砍砍砍」。同時，巫婆對提姆作出了一個提議。

巫婆 嘿，小子。妳要不要看看糖果屋裡面長怎麼樣呢？（然後她轉向巨人）你也來！或許我會想起來如何幫你。
提姆決定冒險去探一下糖果屋。

小矮人#4　喔不，那男孩消失了！
因為天色漸暗，黑森林會變危險，小矮人們決定回家去。

Phrases & Sentence Patterns 慣用語 & 句型

❶ What is done is done. 木已成舟

❷ I am flattered. 過獎了

❸ show off 炫耀

❹ get into a debate 辯論

❺ lest 唯恐；以免

❻ make an offer 提議

❼ Would you like to + 原形動詞？（對他人提議時的客氣用法）你（您）要不要⋯呢？

❽ take the risk 冒險

Cultural Note

Wicked is one of the Broadway shows you don't want to miss when visiting New York City. It's an enjoyable musical that can have you laughing with the characters one minute, then feeling sad the next as they sing stories about love, friendship, and trust. Inspired by The Wizard of Oz, the story depicts the life of two girls, Elphaba and Glinda. While Elphaba was born green-skinned, Glinda is beautiful and popular. They become roommates at school by chance and grow to become good friends. When they meet the Wizard of Oz, Elphaba is tricked into doing something bad to the Wizard's monkey servants. Elphaba soon discovers a secret plan to enslave the animals of Oz. When she refuses to continue to work with the Wizard, rumors are spread through Oz labeling Elphaba as the 'Wicked Witch of the West'. On the other hand, her friend Glinda becomes known as 'Glinda the Good'. After extensive conflict and argument, Glinda eventually discovers the truth and helps Elphaba run away and frees the animals.

文化角落

　　來紐約玩時絕對不會想錯過百老匯的「邪惡女巫」（Wicked）這部劇，這部有趣的音樂劇可以讓你前一秒跟著角色們大笑，下一秒聽著他們唱關於愛情、友情，和信任的歌曲而感到悲傷。故事靈感來自『綠野仙蹤』，描述艾爾法芭（Elphaba）和格琳妲（Glinda）這兩個女孩的人生。艾爾法芭（Elphaba）一出生就是全身綠綠的，而格琳妲（Glinda）則是長得漂亮又受歡迎，她們偶然地在學校成為室友，慢慢變成好朋友，當她們見到綠野仙蹤的巫師時，艾爾法芭（Elphaba）受騙而對巫師的猴子僕人做了不好的事，很快地，她發現有個秘密的計畫正在進行，目的是奴役綠野仙蹤裡的動物，她拒絕和巫師合作，於是謠言開始在綠野仙蹤傳開，艾爾法芭（Elphaba）被稱為「西方壞女巫」，另一方面，格琳特（Glinda）則是「好格林妲」，經過漫長的衝突與爭執之後，格琳特（Glinda）最後發現真相，她協助艾爾法芭（Elphaba）逃走以及釋放所有動物。

In the Candy House.

| Witch | Have a seat here. Hansel and Gretel, please bring some cookies and drinks for our guests. |

Hansel and Gretel bring over a various selection of cookies and soft drinks.

| Witch | Please help yourself. |

| Tim | Thank you. I think I will pass this time. I am on a diet. (*He talks to himself.*) You can't trick me with your cookies. |

| Witch | All kids have a sweet tooth. You have to try some! |

| Giant | (*stuffing his month with two lemon bars*) Definitely! |

| Tim | Not me... |

Witch (*mumbling to herself*) I guess I need to try harder to know what he likes. (*She turns to Tim.*) How about this tasty cinnamon roll? Trust me! After you eat it, you will feel great!

Tim (*shaking his head*) I hate to spoil your appetite, but check out the number of calories in a single cinnamon roll. (*He shows the Witch his calorie calculator app on his phone.*) It has OVER 700 calories!

Witch Oh, my goodness. I had no idea that cinnamon rolls were so unhealthy.

Tim It is a lot of calories! My grandma loves sweets. But after using this app, she is able to resist her craving for sweets most of the time.

Witch I see... you are too aware of the calories you eat!

Tim My mom makes lots of cupcakes and cookies, so I guess I am immune to sweets.

Tim shows the Witch pictures of his mom's desserts.

Witch	Hmmm... your mom is a good baker. Can I have some of her recipes to try out?
Tim	Only if you stop asking me to eat your sweets.
Witch	(*sighing in defeat*) All right my dearie.
Tim	(*showing the Witch the blog where his mom shares her recipes*) My mom is actually a famous baker. (*He hands her his iPhone.*) Here you go, you can check out all the recipes you like.

Soon, the Witch becomes engaged in viewing all the recipes.

第四場

在糖果屋裡

巫婆	請坐。漢賽爾和葛麗特,請拿一些餅乾和飲料來招待客人。漢賽爾和葛麗特拿了各式各樣選擇的餅乾和(無酒精)飲料過來。
巫婆	別客氣,請享用。
提姆	謝謝。我想我這次就不吃了。我正在節食。(自言自語)你沒有辦法用餅乾騙到我的。
巫婆	所有的小孩都愛吃甜的,你一定要試一些!

巨人　（嘴巴裡塞了兩個檸檬蛋糕棒）絕對要試看看的！

提姆　我不用…

巫婆　（輕聲碎碎念）我猜我需要更加把勁知道他喜歡什麼。
（她轉向提姆）要不要試看看這好吃的肉桂捲呢？相信
我！你吃了之後會覺得很棒！

提姆　（搖搖頭）我真的不想要打壞你的胃口，但是看一下一個
肉桂捲的卡路里吧。（他給巫婆看手機上應用程式的卡路
里計算器）這一個就超過 700 卡耶！

巫婆　喔，我的天啊！我完全不知道肉桂捲這麼不健康。

提姆　的確超高卡路里的。我奶奶愛吃甜食，不過用了這應用程
式之後，她大多時候都可以抵抗對甜食的渴望。

巫婆　原來如此…你太在意自己吃進去的卡路里了！

提姆　我媽媽做很多杯子蛋糕和餅乾，所以我猜我已經對甜食免
疫了。
提姆給巫婆看他媽媽做的甜點的照片。

巫婆　恩～你媽媽是烘焙高手。我可以跟她要一些食譜試看看嗎？

提姆　只要你別再要我吃你的甜食。

巫婆　（感到被擊敗，嘆了口氣）好吧，親愛的。

提姆　（給巫婆看他媽媽部落格上面的食譜）我媽媽其實是很有
名的烘焙師。（他將 iPhone 遞給巫婆）拿去吧，你可以

看看所有你喜歡的食譜。

很快地，巫婆全神貫注地瀏覽所有的食譜。

Phrases & Sentence Patterns慣用語 & 句型

❶ Please help yourself. (招待客人時的用語) 別客氣，請盡情享用。

❷ I'll pass this time. (謝絕對方的邀約或好意時) 這次我就不用／不吃／不跟等

❸ On a diet 節食

❹ Sweet tooth 嗜吃甜食 (尤指糖果和巧克力)

❺ How about +名詞／動名詞？ (用於提出建議) …如何呢？例如 "How about going shopping later today?"

❻ hate to + 原形動詞…，but… 不想／不願意…但…

❼ crave for 渴望

❽ be immune to 免疫的；不受影響的

Cultural Note

Cookies and pastries are very common desserts in the U.S households. You can easily find these sweet treats in any supermarket or shopping mall. Restaurants like to offer package deals to their customers, so they can enjoy a dessert after their entree. For example, when you order a meal at Panera Bread, you have the opportunity to buy a pastry from the bakery for only an additional US $0.99. You can select from a variety of pastries, including a chocolate brownie, a piece of pecan pie, a chocolate chip cookie, a blueberry scone, and so on. This type of a package deal at such an affordable price is difficult to resist, especially for people with a sweet tooth! Actually, many pastries might even be tasty to those who don't care for desserts. The only downside is that you'll pay the price of consuming too many calories by only paying US $0.99. This 'deal' can be a real nuisance to people trying to lose weight.

文化角落

　　餅乾和糕點是美國家庭裡很常見的點心，也很容易在任何超市或購物中心找到這些甜食，餐廳也喜歡提供套餐優惠讓客人在吃完主餐之後，可以享受點心。舉例來說，當你在 *Panera Bread*（美國一家以三明治和麵包烘焙為主的連鎖店）點餐時，就有機會多花美金 99 分從烘焙部選一樣麵包糕點，選擇非常多樣，包括巧克力布朗尼、一片胡桃派、巧克力碎片餅乾、藍莓司康等等，像這類價格親民的套餐優惠讓人難以抗拒，尤其是愛吃甜食的人！其實，很多麵包糕點甚至連不嗜甜點的人都可能覺得非常可口，唯一的缺點是，你只需要花美金不到一塊錢（99 分）就輕易吃進過多卡路里，對於正想減肥的人來說，還真是麻煩事。

With the Witch using his phone, Tim takes out his digital camera and looks at the photos of the Seven Dwarfs. Meanwhile, Hansel and Gretel are ready to leave for a friend's graduation party.

Gretel   We are about to leave.

Witch   Oh, I almost forgot. Did you pack some cookies for the party?

Hansel   Of course we did!

Witch   Great! Have fun! By the way, don't forget to invite your friends over to visit our Candy House.

Hansel and Gretel   As you wish.

Tim   I should take off too.

Witch   Oh, no. Please stay. I would love to have some company after they leave. I have very comfy guest rooms that will make you feel as snug as a bug in a rug.

Tim Thanks for the offer but I got to go home now.

Witch I must insist.

Tim No thank you. (*He thinks to himself.*) I will be the focus of the next Amber Alert if I don't get home soon.

Witch (*Her face turns red with frustration.*) PLEASE STAY...

Tim nervously rummages through his backpack, trying to find anything to change the subject. Then, he thinks of his digital camera he's still holding.

Tim Oh, look, this was the photo I just took earlier. I love your smile!

Witch Thank you. But look at those wrinkles on my forehead.

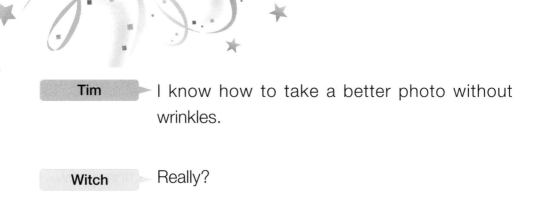

Tim — I know how to take a better photo without wrinkles.

Witch — Really?

Tim — I can show you. But first you need to close your eyes.

While the Witch was closing her eyes for another photo, Tim quickly grabs his iPhone off the table and quietly sneaks out of the Candy House.

Five minutes, later...

Witch — Are you done yet? (*She opens her eyes.*) Grrr... where did that kid go? I've been tricked! (*She turns to the Giant.*) Why are YOU still here?

Pacing around the house in frustration, the Witch hears a knock at the door.

Witch — Oh, that must be Tim returning after wandering in the Dark Forest.

The Witch opens the door and sees a gigantic woman bending her head down to look at her.

Giant's Wife	Excuse me. Have you seen my husband?

Witch	(*pointing at the little guy eating cookies by the table.*) Please get him out of my house.

正當巫婆在使用他的 iPhone 時，提姆拿出數位相機看起照片裡的七個小矮人。同時間，漢賽爾和葛麗特準備出發去一個朋友的畢業派對。

Gretel	我們差不多要離開了。

巫婆	喔，我差點忘掉了。你們有打包一些餅乾帶去派對嗎？

Hansel	當然有囉！

巫婆	太棒了！好好玩！對了，別忘了邀請你們的朋友到糖果屋來玩。

漢賽爾&葛麗特	如你所願。

提姆	我也該走了。

巫婆	喔，不。請留下，他們離開之後我想要有個伴陪。我有很舒適的客房，你會一夜都好眠的。

提姆	謝謝你的好意，不過我現在該回家了。

巫婆 我堅持。

提姆 不，謝了。（他心想）我再不趕快回家就會變成下一個安柏警報（Amber Alert）的主角吧。

巫婆 （臉因沮喪而變紅）拜託請留下來。
提姆緊張地在他背包亂翻，想要找到任何可以改變話題的東西，然後忽然想到他手上的數位相機。

提姆 喔，你瞧，這是我剛剛拍的照片。喔～我愛死你那微笑了！

巫婆 謝謝。不過你看看我額頭那些皺紋。

提姆 我知道如何拍出更好、沒有皺紋的照片。

巫婆 真的嗎？

提姆 我可以秀給你看。不過為了拍這張照，妳得先閉上眼睛。
當巫婆閉上雙眼等拍照時，提姆快速地拿了桌上的iPhone 並且安靜地偷溜出糖果屋。

五分鐘後…

巫婆 你拍好了嗎？（她睜開雙眼）啊～那小孩去哪裡了？啊…我被耍了！（她轉向巨人）你怎麼還在這裡？
巫婆因為挫敗在房子裡來回走動一陣子後，聽到了敲門聲。

提姆 喔，一定是提姆在黑森林遊蕩後調頭回來了。
巫婆打開門，看到一個體型巨大的女人彎著頭看著她。

巨人的老婆　不好意思，您有看到我先生嗎？

巫婆　（指著正在桌子旁吃著餅乾的小個子）麻煩將他帶走。

Phrases & Sentence Patterns 慣用語 & 句型

❶ leave for 前往

❷ be about to + 原形動詞：即將做什麼；正打算做什麼

❸ as you wish 如你所願

❹ Take off 離開（某個地方，聚會活動等）；（飛機）起飛

❺ would love to + 原形動詞：（常用於表示請求）想（要）…

❻ as snug as a bug in a rug 非常舒適又安全（註解：想像自己像飛蛾幼蟲一樣，很舒服的在捲起來的地毯裡睡覺）

❼ Thanks for the offer（通常用在接受或拒絕對方的提議或幫忙時）謝謝你的好意

❽ Amber alert 美國一個走失孩童的全國通報系統，只要持有手機的人都會自動收到有關失蹤孩童的訊息，期望提高尋獲的機率。

Cultural Note

In the U.S., there are many parties held for kids. A baby's first birthday is always a big thing. The parents will send out party invitations to their family and friends. The hosts serve food and refreshments at the party and guests typically bring gifts for the birthday boy/girl. The highlight of the party is when the baby is given his/her first cake, smashing it and making a mess. Another feature is when the parents open gifts one by one and express how cute/great each gift is. In addition to birthday's parties, another significant party is the graduation party when the kid graduates from high school. It's common to send an invitation card with a professional photo or two of the kid. This party celebrates the kid's completion of an important stage in life and introduces them to the bigger world ahead. Instead of bringing gifts, guests typically bring a card with cash or a gift card inside. After all, it is expensive to enter college and start life as an adult.

Act One Scene 5

文化角落

　　美國有很多專為孩子舉辦的派對，滿周歲生日派對一直都是一件大事，父母會郵寄派對邀請卡給親朋好友，派對上會提供食物與飲料，客人照慣例會帶生日禮物給壽星，派對的高潮即是，當寶寶拿到人生第一個蛋糕時，開始捏碎蛋糕，搞得一團亂，另一個重頭戲則是父母一一拆開生日禮物，並表達每個禮物是多麼可愛或多麼棒。除了生日派對之外，另一個具有重大意義的派對是小孩從高中畢業時所舉辦的畢業派對，邀請卡上通常會放上一兩張畢業生的沙龍照，這派對是要慶祝小孩完成人生很重要的一個階段，邁向人生前方更寬闊的世界，受邀請的客人不再帶禮物，而是帶張卡片並在信封裡附上現金或禮卡，畢竟，上大學和展開成人的生活是很昂貴的。

Run, Forest, Run

Wizard: (watching Tim's adventure through his Crystal Ball.) Very impressive. He has dealt with the Witch in such a clever way. But the dark force is growing. I need to speed up his training. Hmmm... I think it's time for him to meet the girls.

The Wizard wiggles his magic wand and leads Tim to the girls in the Dark Forest.

Scene 1

Tim is lost in the Dark Forest. There is nothing but trees as far as the eye can see. He hears the sound of horses galloping in the distance. Snow White is coming towards him.

Snow White (*out of breath*) Excuse me. If anybody asks you, please don't tell them you saw me.

Tim (*with excitement*) You're Snow White!

Snow White How do you know my name? Oh, no! Are you one of them?

Tim No, don't worry. I've heard a lot about your grace and beauty.

Snow White Oh my, that's very kind of you. I hate to be rude, but I really need to go now.

Tim What happened? Is there anything I can do to help?

Snow White — Well, it's a long story. In short, I broke my stepmother's magical mirror, and she is very upset with me.

Tim — Oh, I don't blame you for being in such a hurry.

Snow White — It's just that the mirror kept annoying me by saying that my stepmother was the fairest one of all. This morning, as I was arguing with the man in the mirror, I was so frustrated that I threw my brush and broke it by accident.

Tim — Well, out of sight, out of mind. I bet your stepmother is VERY angry.

Snow White — Tell me about it!

Tim and Snow White hear horses coming towards them.

Snow White — Oh no, I think they are approaching. Nice chatting with you.

However, it is too late. Snow White and Tim get caught and are taken away by The Queen's Knights.
In the Queen's castle.

The Queen → Snow White, this is the third magical mirror you broke. Do you have any idea how hard it is to make a magical mirror?

Snow White → Mother, I am sorry, but I just got so angry at the mirror.

The Queen → Young lady, you need to learn to control your temper. This time, you will take care of my apple trees as punishment.

Snow White → Yes, Mother.

The Queen → (*turning to Tim*) Now, who are you?

Tim → (*nervously*) Your Majesty, I am Tim BeauDaring.

第二幕

跑呀，在森林裡，跑呀

　　巫師：（從水晶球看提姆的冒險）表現不錯，他處理巫婆的方式還挺聰明的，不過黑暗勢力漸長，我必須加速他的受訓過程。恩⋯我想是時候讓他見見女孩子們了。

巫師搖了一下他的魔棒並引導正在黑森林的提姆，往遇見女孩子們的方向前進。

提姆在黑森林裡迷路了。眼前所及除了樹什麼都沒有看到。他聽到遠方傳來馬匹疾馳的聲音，白雪公主正朝他的方向前進。

白雪公主 （喘不過氣來）不好意思，如果有人問起，請不要説你見過我。

提姆 （感到興奮）你是白雪公主！

白雪公主 你怎麼知道我的名字？喔，不，你是他們的其中一員嗎？

提姆 不是，別擔心。我是久仰你的優雅與美貌。

白雪公主 哎呀，你人真好。我實在不想要失禮，不過我真的該走了。

提姆 發生什麼事？有我可以幫忙的地方嗎？

白雪公主 那個，真是一言難盡，簡言之，我打破我後母的魔鏡，她現在非常不高興。

提姆 喔，那我不會怪你這麼急著走。

白雪公主 只是因為那鏡子一直煩我，説我後母是世界上最美的。今天早上，當我在和鏡中人爭辯時，我實在太沮喪了，於是我對鏡子丟了梳子，就意外地把它打破了。

Act Two　Scene 1

| 提姆 | 恩，眼不見為淨囉。我敢說你後母現在非常的生氣吧。 |

| 白雪公主 | 當然了！
提姆和白雪公主聽到馬匹正朝他們逼近。 |

| 白雪公主 | 喔不，我想他們逼近了。很高興和你聊上幾句。
然而，為時已晚，白雪公主和提姆被逮到了，並一起被皇后的騎士帶走。 |

在皇后的城堡裡

| 皇后 | 白雪公主，這已是第三個被你打破的魔鏡了，你知不知道要做一個魔鏡是多困難的嗎？ |

| 白雪公主 | 母后，真的對不起，但我只是對那鏡子感到非常生氣。 |

| 皇后 | 小姐，你需要學著控制自己的脾氣。這次要罰你照顧我的蘋果樹。 |

| 白雪公主 | 是的，母后。 |

| 皇后 | （轉向提姆）說吧，你是何方神聖？ |

| 提姆 | （緊張地）皇后陛下，我是提姆・博德林（Tim BeauDaring）。 |

Phrases & Sentence Patterns 慣用語 & 句型

❶ in the distance 在遠處

❷ I've heard a lot about you. 久仰大名了

❸ It's a long story. 一言難盡

❹ I don't blame you. 我不會怪你的（意指，我懂你的心情；我懂你為何這麼做）

❺ By accident 意外地

❻ Out of sight, out of mind. 眼不見為淨

❼ I bet 我敢打賭；我敢肯定（猜測）

❽ Tell me about it 完全同意（你的說法／感受等）

Cultural Note

The title of this Act "Run, Forest, Run" is inspired by the movie Forrest Gump (1994). The movie, starring Tom Hanks, is the life story of a young man, Forrest Gump, and the people he encounters. One-day Gump encounters some bullies throwing rocks. His best friend, Jenny, shouts, "Run, Forrest, Run!" so he can get away. Another famous quote is "Life was like a box of chocolates. You never know what you're gonna get." It makes sense when we think about how life surprises us all the time. The movie cleverly weaves the major events from the second half of the 20th century in the United States into Forrest Gump's life, such as the African-American Civil Rights Movement, Assassination of John F. Kennedy, and the Vietnam War. Oh, when you visit the Navy Pier in Chicago, don't forget to visit the Bubba Gump Shrimp Co., which is a restaurant themed after one scene in the movie!

文化角落

　　這一幕標題「跑呀，在森林裡，跑呀」的靈感是來自電影「阿甘正傳」（1994），由湯姆漢克斯（*Tom Hanks*）主演，描述佛瑞特斯阿甘（*Forrest Gump*）這年輕人和他所遇見的人的人生故事，有一天，阿甘碰到一些霸凌他的人丟他石頭，他最好的朋友珍妮（*Jenny*）為了讓他逃走，對他大喊著：「快跑，佛瑞斯特，快跑！」另一個有名的台詞是「人生就像是一盒巧克力，你永遠不知道你吃到的是什麼口味。」電影很巧妙地將美國 20 世紀後半期的主要事件都穿插在阿甘的人生裡，像是美國黑人的民權運動、甘迺迪總統遭暗殺事件，和越戰。對了，如果有機會拜訪芝加哥的海軍碼頭（*Navy Pier*），別忘了去試試 *Bubba Gump Shrimp Co.* 這家以電影裡其中一個情節為主題的餐廳。

The Queen ➤ Why is a young lad like you wandering in the forest with my daughter?

Tim ➤ Your Majesty. I've never met her until today.

The Queen ➤ All her ex-boyfriends told me the same thing when I caught them with her in the forest.

Tim ➤ Look at me. Snow White is totally out of my league.

The Queen ➤ I'd really like to believe you and be a merciful Queen. But as the mother of a princess, I must protect her pure and innocent image. Now that I have revealed Snow White's dating history with a slip of my tongue, sorry, you must be silenced.

Tim ➤ I promise that I won't tell a soul. I am a man of my word.

The Queen ➤ (*shaking her head with a look of disbelief*) I've been deceived by men's words too many times.

Tim — (*trying to get out of the situation*.) Your Majesty, you are too smart for me to deceive you!

The Queen — That is true, but to protect her reputation, you will be either thrown in jail for life or put to death tomorrow. Which one do you prefer?

Tim — (*hesitantly*) Ja-a-a-il?

The Queen — Fine. Jail first, then death.

The guards take Tim to the dungeon.

Tim — (*mumbling to himself*) This is not looking good. I was stupid to put myself in danger. (*He jumps suddenly and feels a chill in his spine.*) What's that moving over there?

In the dim light, he sees two mice passing through a small hole in the wall. He takes out a flashlight from his backpack to see where they are going. He sees something inside the hole.

Tim — (*reaching one hand into the hole*) Stupid mouse, stop tickling my hand!

He pulls out a rolled-up piece of paper, unrolls it and starts to read.

第二場

皇后 為什麼你一個年輕小伙子和我女兒在森林裡遊蕩？

提姆 皇后陛下，我到今天才遇到她。

皇后 她所有的前男友被我抓到和她一起在森林裡時，也是跟你說一樣的話。

提姆 看看我，我配不上白雪公主。

皇后 我真的很想要相信你的話並當一個仁慈的皇后，可是身為公主的母后，我必須保護她純潔無暇的形象。既然我不小心說溜嘴，透露了白雪公主的戀愛史，真是抱歉，你必須被解決掉以封住嘴巴。

提姆 我保證我絕對會保密到底，我是說到做到的人。

皇后 （面帶懷疑的搖搖頭）我被男人的話騙過太多次了。

提姆 （試著脫身）陛下，您這麼冰雪聰明我怎麼有辦法欺騙您呢！

皇后 這倒是真的，不過為了保護她的名聲，你必須被終生監禁或是明天立刻處死，你比較中意哪個？

| 提姆 | （遲疑地説）被－關－起－來？ |

| 皇后 | 行。那先關起來再處死。 |

侍衛將提姆帶到地窖。

| 提姆 | （自言自語）情況不太妙，我怎麼會笨到讓自己陷入險境。（他忽然跳了起來，背脊傳來一陣涼意。）那邊有什麼在動？
在微弱的燈光下，他看到兩隻老鼠穿過牆上一個小洞。他從背包拿出手電筒往老鼠去的方向照，他看到洞裡有個東西。 |

| 提姆 | （一隻手伸進洞裡）笨鼠，不要再搔我癢啦！
他拿出一個捲起來的紙張，打開它開始唸。 |

Phrases & Sentence Patterns慣用語 & 句型

❶ out of someone's league 配不上（尤其是想要追求的對象某些條件遠比追求者好時，像是對方是學校風雲人物，富二代等，朋友可能就會説，別傻了，「你高攀不上」，「你追不到的」之類的戲謔話。）

❷ slip of one's tongue 説溜嘴

❸ will not tell a soul 誓言保密

❹ a man of one's word 説到做到

❺ for life 終生

❻ put to death 處死；判死刑

❼ put someone in danger 使陷入險境

❽ feel the chill in one's spine 背脊一陣涼意

In the first version of the story Snow White, the princess was named Snowdrop. Before she was born, the Queen was sitting by a window with a black window frame, watching the snow falling down from the sky. Then, she cut her finger and a few drops of blood fell onto the snow. She looked at what happened and thought that perhaps her girl would be as white as snow, as red as her blood, and as black as the window frame. Therefore, in movies, Snow White always has snowy white skin, beautiful long black hair and rosy red checks. By the way, when it comes to Snow White, everyone knows the famous words from the Queen: "Mirror, mirror on the wall, who's the fairest one of all?" Well, it's so catchy that you can create your own for fun, such as "Mirror, mirror on the wall, who's the coolest one of all?" Can you make up your own?

文化角落

　　在最初版的「白雪公主」故事當中，公主的名字是「雪花公主」（Snowdrop），在她出生之前，王后坐在有黑色窗框的窗邊，看著雪從天空飄下來，然後她不小心割傷手指，幾滴鮮血滴在雪上，她看了看，心想，或許她的女兒會像白雪一樣白，鮮血一樣紅，窗框一樣黑。因此，在電影中，白雪公主的形象一直都是如雪般的白色肌膚，美麗的烏黑秀髮，和蘋果紅的雙頰。對了，每次一提到「白雪公主」，人人都會想到王后那經典名言：「牆上的魔鏡啊，魔鏡，誰是世界上最美麗的？」也因為這句話很朗朗上口，你可以創造自己的搞笑版本，像是「牆上的魔鏡啊，魔鏡，誰是世界上最酷的？」你可以現在就編一個嗎？

Tim is reading the unrolled piece of paper.

To Whom It May Concern:

You're reading this note because you were caught with Snow White. (Suddenly, a big mouth pops out of the paper inches from Tim's face staring him and shouts.) YOU FOOL! DON'T EVER GET CAUGHT! Anyway, that is the last thing we should be discussing now. Since you did find this note, perhaps your stupidity is not totally incurable. Now, ask me how to get you out of here.

Tim   Can you PLEASE tell me how I get out of here?
Pretty please, with sugar on top!

*(The big mouth pops out again.) Is that all you got!? Get creative!
You're in a fairy tale world! SING IT like you mean it!*

Tim   *(singing out of tune)* I sit alone in the darkness
of my lonely room... lalala... I want to be free
free. Free -ee-ee-ee. ('I Want To Be Free' by
Elvis.)

*(A satisfying smile shows.) Dude, you're an old soul. Very well. Here
it is! "What does The Queen like the most?"*

Tim   That is a *riddle*, not a solution!!!
*(A sarcastic mouth speaks.) Use your
IMAGINATION! Adios!*

*The paper disappears from Tim's hands. The guards enter to take Tim
to The Queen.*

The Queen   Do you have any last words before you die?

Tim   Wait, if you promise to let me go, I will show
you the most powerful magical mirror in the

world. You will look like the fairest one of all no matter how old you are.

The Queen (*suspiciously*) Really? All right, I will give you one last chance. Show me.
Tim quickly downloads a photo-editing app to his Smart Phone.

Tim Ok, now look at my phone and smile.
He snaps a photo and shows the Queen how to edit it in the photo-editing app.

Tim See, with this app you can make your wrinkles and dark circles disappear! You can even adjust your skin tone!

The Queen Wow! This is really mind blowing!

 第三場

提姆正在唸打開的紙。

敬啟者：

　　你正在唸這信條因為你被抓到和白雪公主在一起。（突然一張大嘴巴從紙上蹦出來在提姆的面前大叫，嚇到提姆。）你這笨蛋！絕對不要被抓到！反正，這是目

前我們最需要討論的事情了，即然你有辦法找到這紙條，或許你的愚蠢還不到完全無藥可救。現在，先問我你該如何逃離這裡。

提姆　可以拜託你跟我說如何逃離這裡嗎？拜託，千萬個拜託！
（大嘴巴再度蹦出來）你就只有這麼點本事嗎？你在童話故事裡頭耶！用你的真心唱出來！

提姆　（五音不全地唱著）在我孤單的房間裡我獨自坐在黑暗當中…啦啦啦…我想要自由、自由、自～由～（貓王的歌「我想要自由」）
（一張滿意的笑容蹦了出來）老兄，你有個老靈魂。很好！接招「皇后最喜歡什麼？」

提姆　這是個謎語，不是解答啊！
（一張嘲笑的嘴巴說）請用你的想像力！再會！
紙張從提姆的手上消失了。侍衛進來將提姆帶去見皇后。

皇后　在你死前有什麼遺言嗎？

提姆　等等，如果您答應放我走，我就給你看全世界魔力最強的鏡子，不管您幾歲看起來都會是全世界最美的。

皇后　（懷疑地）真的嗎？好吧，給你最後一次機會，秀給我看。
提姆快速地下載一個美圖應用程式到他的智慧型手機裡。

提姆　好了，現在看著我的電話並且笑一個。
他拍了一張照並展示給皇后看，該如何在修圖應用程式裡修照片。

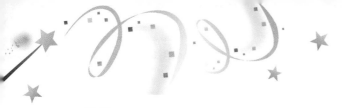

提姆 您瞧，有了這個應用程式之後，您可以消除臉上的皺紋和黑眼圈！甚至可以調整膚色！

皇后 哇！這真的太令人驚豔了！

Phrases & Sentence Patterns慣用語 & 句型

❶ To Whom It May Concern（書信格式）敬啟者；致有關人士

❷ The last thing 最不重要的事

❸ Pretty please, with sugar on top！拜託，千萬個拜託（加糖代表「額外」的意思，就像喝咖啡時會額外加糖讓咖啡喝起來更加好喝，所以這裡的 sugar on top 是強調語氣。）

❹ Is that all you got? 你就只有這麼一點本事嗎？

❺ 原形動詞+ it + like you mean it. 發自內心的去做某事（常用動詞 say,或 do, 來表示某人說或做的時候是發自內心想這麼做的）

❻ out of tune 五音不全；不成調

❼ old soul 一個老靈魂（可用來形容一個人對於比自己當代還久遠的人事物感興趣或甚至非常熟悉）

❽ Something is mind blowing. 太令人驚豔了！太令人印象深刻了！

Cultural Note

The songs "Love Me Tender" and "I Can't Help Falling In Love With You" used to be, and probably still are, two of the more popular songs an English teacher introduces in her/his English class. Both songs have simple lyrics and a slow rhythm to please English learners' ears. The original was sung by Elvis Presley (1/8/1935 - 8/16/1977), who is regarded as the most influential rock 'n' roll icons of the twentieth century popular culture. Even today, he continues to be missed by his fans all over the world. Graceland, former home of Elvis, is a mansion in Memphis, Tennessee. It currently serves as a museum and is an important tourist site in Memphis. In addition to Graceland, the influence of Elvis is still everywhere in Memphis. Wherever you go, you can find stores selling souvenirs about Elvis! Unlike some cities in the U.S., which can be hot but dry in summer, you will find Memphis just as hot and humid as you feel during summers in Taiwan!

　　「溫柔的愛我」和「情不自禁愛上你」曾經是（或許現在依舊是）英文老師很喜歡在課堂上介紹的其中兩首非常受歡迎的歌。這兩首歌的歌詞簡單，旋律慢，很適合播放給英文學習者聽。原唱貓王（*Elvis Presley*）（1/8/1935-8/16/1977）被認為是 20 世紀最具影響力的搖滾樂巨星，即便到今日，全世界的歌迷依舊懷念他。貓王故居優雅園（*Graceland*）位於田納西州（*Tennessee*）的夢菲斯（*Memphis*），目前為博物館，是當地非常重要的觀光景點，除了優雅園（*Graceland*）之外，也可以在夢菲斯（*Memphis*）感受到貓王無所不在的影響力，所到之處，都可以很容易找到有關他的紀念品！不像美國其他城市，夏天時一般都是熱但乾燥，夢菲斯（*Memphis*）這城市的夏天可能會讓你感受到和台灣一樣悶熱的氣候。

Scene 4

MP3 09

Tim takes out another smart phone from his backpack that has the photo-editing app installed. Then he gives it to the Queen as a gift. Overjoyed by Tim's amazing magical mirror, the Queen sets him free. She provides him with a beautiful white horse to take him home. Tim rides for a little while before bumping into the Giant in the Dark Forest.

Tim ▸ Hey, what's up?

Giant ▸ Not much... well, I was running away from my angry wife. She is NOT happy that I ate all those cookies and was shrunk by the Witch!

Tim ▸ Poor you. You should stand up for yourself!

Giant ▸ Easier said than done, kid.

Tim ▸ Let me give you a ride. C'mon up!

Giant ▸ *(trying to jump onto the horse, but his effort is in vain)* Well... isn't this frustrating. Before I go home, I need to figure out how to transform back to my original size.

| Tim | Give me your hand and I'll pull you up. I am heading home. Perhaps my family doctor knows how to solve your problem. |

After a while, Tim and the Giant run into a rabbit at a fork in the road.

| Mr. Rabbit | (*shouting*) Watch where you're going! Your horse almost head-butted me! |

| Tim | Wow, you're a talking rabbit! |

| Mr. Rabbit | Of course rabbits can talk! (*He looks at his pocket watch*) Oh, I'm running late. I'm gonna lose the bet again. |

| Tim | Wait a minute! Are you Mr. Rabbit from "Alice in Wonderland" ? |

| Mr. Rabbit | Who's Alice? Anyway, I gotta go! I'm racing the turtle. |

| Giant | Huh, that was YOU who fell asleep under the tree and lost the contest! |

Mr. Rabbit — That certainly spread quickly through the grapevine, didn't it? Well, this time I'm bound and determined to regain my reputation.

Tim — Good luck!

Mr. Rabbit — Oh, no! I've forgotten which road to take!

Tim — What's your destination? I can help you find your way with my GPS, as long as we can get a signal here. Wow! We have a very good connection! Amazing!

After Tim shows Mr. Rabbit the route on the GPS, Mr. Rabbit promises to return the favor at a later time before he speeds away down the road.

第四場

　　提姆從背包拿出另一個已安裝好美圖編輯應用程式的智慧型手機，並將它送給皇后當禮物。因為非常高興拿到提姆這令人驚喜的魔鏡，皇后釋放了他，並給他一匹白色駿馬帶他回家。提姆在黑森林騎馬騎了一陣子後碰到了巨人。

提姆 ▸ 嘿，你好？

巨人 ▸ 沒啥事…恩，其實我是在逃離我那生氣的老婆，她真的很不高興我吃了巫婆的那些餅乾之後就被縮小了！

提姆 ▸ 真可憐，你應該捍衛自己的權利。

巨人 ▸ 小子，這說的比做的容易。

提姆 ▸ 讓我載你一程，上來吧！

巨人 ▸ （試著跳上馬，但他的努力卻徒勞無功。）哎呀…也未免太令人沮喪了。在我回家前，我必須找到變回原本身材的方法。

提姆 ▸ 手給我，我拉你上來。我正在回家的路上，或許我的家庭醫生知道如何解決你的問題。
過一陣子，提姆和巨人在一條岔路碰到一隻兔子。

兔子先生 ▸ （大叫）看路啊！你的馬差點和我迎頭相撞。

提姆 ▸ 哇，你是會說話的兔子！

兔子先生 ▸ 兔子當然會說話！（他看一看自己的懷錶）喔，我要遲到了，打賭又會輸了。

提姆 ▸ 等一下！你是「愛麗絲夢遊仙境」裡的那隻兔子嗎？

兔子先生 ▸ 誰是愛麗絲？總之，我該走了！我正在和烏龜賽跑。

Act Two Scene 4

巨人 ▶ 阿哈，就是你在樹下睡覺然後輸了比賽！

兔子先生 ▶ 壞事果然傳千里，是不是啊？那個，這一次我吃了秤砣鐵
了心，一定會恢復我的名聲。

提姆 ▶ 祝你好運！

兔子先生 ▶ 喔不！我忘了該走哪條路了！

提姆 ▶ 你的目的地是哪裡？我可以用我的衛星導航（GPS）幫
你找路，只要這裡收得到訊號的話。哇！這裡的收訊很好
耶！太驚人了！
提姆給兔子先生看衛星導航上的路線之後，兔子先生在趕
路之前，保證日後會回報他。

Phrases & Sentence Patterns慣用語 & 句型

❶ bump into 巧遇

❷ Stand up for yourself. 捍衛自己（=defend yourself）

❸ Something is easier said than done.說比做容易

❹ in vain 徒勞無功

❺ fork in the road 岔路

❻ through the grapevine 從傳聞中聽說；聽小道消息知道

❼ bound and determined 吃了秤砣鐵了心；堅決的

❽ as long as 只要

A man is in a car accident, and his car is damaged. A police officer asks him if he needs an ambulance. The man suddenly stands up and says," Nope. I can walk to the hospital on my own." Then he limps away. This is a sarcastic story to express how expensive it is to see a doctor in the U.S. In Taiwan, because of the National Health Insurance, medical costs are affordable to most people. In the U.S., people need to arrange their own medical insurance. However, since every policy is different, the fee for the same treatment can vary significantly. Thus, people typically do not go to the doctor for little illnesses, such as a cold. It is also common to make an appointment several months in advance. However, no matter what policy people have, the charge for going to the emergency room or getting a ride in an ambulance will definitely cost a fortune!

文化角落

　　有一個人出了車禍，車子毀了。警察問他要不要叫救護車，這人忽然站起來說：「不用了，我可以自己走路到醫院。」然後一跛一跛走了。這個笑話是在諷刺在美國看醫生所需付出的昂貴醫藥費。在台灣，因為有健保，大多數的人都負擔得起醫療費用，在美國，則需要自己買好醫療保險，然而，既然每個保險方案不盡相同，同樣的治療所需負擔的費用可以相差十萬八千里。因此，一般來說，像是感冒之類的小病一般是不會想去看醫生的，另一個普遍的現象是要提早幾個月就掛號。不過，無論買的是哪家的保險，去急診室或是叫救護車的費用是絕對非常昂貴的！

After Tim and the Giant ride for a while, the horse stops suddenly and starts sniffing at some bushes.

Cinderella — (*coming out of the bushes*) Hahaha! Stop that you silly horse! I'm ticklish!

Tim — Hello, I'm Tim and this is my friend, the Giant.

Cinderella — Greetings! I'm Cinderella. It's very nice to meet you.

Tim — Cinderella? Nice to meet you too! How come you're hiding in the bushes?

Cinderella — Shhh… I am hiding from King Interfering's Knights.

Tim — King Interfering's Knight?

Cinderella — I married his son, The Prince, last year. King Interfering is my father-in-law.

Tim ▸ Don't you live happily ever after?

Cinderella ▸ (*sighing*) There were many happy moments until my father-in-law started to stick his nose in my business!

Giant ▸ I feel your pain.

Cinderella ▸ Anyway, I attend a book club every week with my girls. But, whenever my prince is on a business trip, my father-in-law won't allow me to leave the castle.

Tim ▸ That's too bad! King Interfering really lives up to his name.

Cinderella ▸ Oh no! I think they're coming. I have to get back into the bushes. Please don't disclose my whereabouts.

Tim ▸ Wait, before you hide can I borrow your white cloak?

Cinderella ▸ Of course! Here you are.

Cinderella hands Tim her cloak and jumps back in the bushes.

> **Tim** (*talking to the Giant*) We have to help her. Can you tie this cloak tightly between these trees and make sure to keep it as flat as possible?

Tim takes the mini-projector out of his backpack, which he is supposed to use to present his research on "The Life of Reptiles" for his science summer camp next week. He points it towards the cloak and images of alligators dragging zebras under water display in the dark night. King Interfering's Knights approach and the horses suddenly rear up when they see the images. The Knights tumble off their horses to the ground and run away in fear.

 第五場

提姆和巨人騎了好一陣子之後，馬忽然停下來，開始聞草叢。

> **灰姑娘** （從草叢裡出來）哈哈哈！你這笨馬別聞了！很癢呢！

> **提姆** 哈囉，我是提姆，這是我的朋友，巨人。

> **灰姑娘** 你們好！我是灰姑娘，很高興認識你們。

> **提姆** 灰姑娘？我也很高興認識你！你為什麼躲在草叢裡呢？

> **灰姑娘** 噓～我在躲愛管閒事王的騎士們。

提姆　愛管閒事王的騎士？

灰姑娘　我去年和他的兒子，也就是王子，結婚了，愛管閒事王是我的公公。

提姆　難道你沒有從此過著幸福快樂的日子嗎？

灰姑娘　（嘆氣）我們有很多快樂的時光直到我公公開始管我的閒事。

巨人　我完全能體會。

灰姑娘　總之，我每週都和姊妹淘開讀書會，可是只要我的王子出差，我公公就不准許我離開城堡。

提姆　真是太糟糕了！愛管閒事王國果然名不虛傳。

灰姑娘　喔不！我想他們來了！我必須躲回草叢裡，請不要透露我的去向。

提姆　等等，在你躲起來之前，可以借給我你白色的披風嗎？

灰姑娘　當然！拿去吧！
灰姑娘遞給提姆她的披風之後又跳進草叢裡。

提姆　（對著巨人說）我們得幫助她。你可以將這披風緊緊地綁在樹之間，務必盡量讓披風表面平整。
提姆從背包拿出小型投影機，他本來是打算在下星期的科學夏令營時，用這投影機做他的口頭報告「爬蟲類的一生」。他將投影機對準披風，一張張鱷魚拖著斑馬進水裡的影像在黑夜中播放著。愛管閒事王的騎士們逼近，馬看

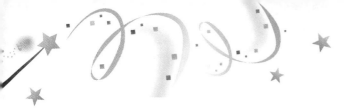

到影像時，忽然前腿往後仰，騎士們從馬上跌落地並害怕地跑走。

Phrases & Sentence Patterns慣用語 & 句型

❶ How come+ 主詞＋動詞…？ 為什麼…？

❷ 稱謂-in-law：用來表示因婚姻而產生的親屬關係，例如 father-in-law 岳父／公公, daughter-in-law 媳婦，以此類推。

❸ Stick someone's nose in one's business. 愛多管閒事

❹ I feel your pain. 感同身受

❺ on a business trip 出差

❻ live up to something 實踐；不辜負

❼ be supposed to + 原形動詞：原本應該…；本來打算…

❽ Rear up 馬匹前腳提起來往後仰的動作

Cultural Note

Independence is an importance value in the U.S. Even before a baby is born, many parents already have the baby room ready for the baby to sleep on his or her own at the very young age. The concept of independence is also noticeable in how Americans view their medical coverage needs. To some extent, because they value their freedom, so it would be very difficult for them to set up a national health Insurance like what the people have in

Taiwan. In addition, when it comes to marriage, once a couple is married they are thought of, and respected as, a family. Parents of both sides tend not to get too involved in the couple's everyday family life. For example, in Taiwan, it is common to have grandparents watching their grandchildren every day. However, this is typically not the situation in the U.S. The parents will tell the couple, "Your children are your responsibility. We have our own plans and can only help out sometimes!"

文化角落

　　獨立在美國是非常重要的價值觀，打從寶寶還未出世之前，很多父母早已準備好嬰兒房，讓嬰兒很小的時候就開始自己睡一間房。獨立這概念也可以從美國人對於醫療給付需求的認知窺探一二。某種程度而言，因為他們重視自由，所以很難像台灣一樣設立一個全民健保制度。此外，以婚姻來說，一對情侶一旦結婚了，就會被視為一個家庭單位，且得到應有的尊重。雙邊父母傾向不太介入小倆口的日常生活，譬如，在台灣我們很常看到祖父母輩每天幫忙帶孫子，然而，這情形在美國就不會是常態，這裡的父母可能會對小倆口說「你們的小孩是你們的責任，我們還有自己的打算，只能偶爾幫忙喔！」

Cinderella Thank you for rescuing me. Can I do anything for you in return?

Tim (*smiling*) No worries.

Giant Oh, maybe you can help me? Do you know how to turn me back into a BIG giant?

Cinderella I'm sorry. I really don't know how... but I might know someone who does! Would you like to come along with me to my book club and ask her in person?

Giant That'd be great! Tim, would you come with us before you travel home?

Tim Sure!

Cinderella *(frustrated)* Oh, no! I put out my torch when I hid in the bushes and I can't relight it! Now I won't be able to identify the secret symbols directing me to the book club.

Tim What do the secret symbols look like?

Cinderella We always mark a small 'R' on the trees along the path to guide the way.

Tim *(taking out a flashlight from his backpack)* Ta-da! Tim to the rescue!

Giant Wow! This torch is bright and it isn't even hot.

Tim Do you want to see something even cooler?

Tim takes a pair of digital night vision binoculars out of his backpack and shows the Giant how to use them.

Giant Cool! I just saw deer over there!

Tim You can help us by watching out for dangerous animals.

Cinderella is riding the horse while Tim and the Giant are leading the way on foot. After traveling for a while, the Giant suddenly stops them and asks them to be quiet.

Giant — Wait! (*He pulls Mr. Rabbit out of the bushes by his long ears.*) Ah! I got him! Look who I found!

Mr. Rabbit — (*kicking his feet in protest*) Put me down!

The Giant puts Mr. Rabbit down.

Tim — It's you again! What's up?

Mr. Rabbit — (*drooping his ears*) I lost the race. The Queen of Hearts flipped her lid!

Cinderella — I'm sorry... but try to stay positive! Every cloud has a silver lining!

Mr. Rabbit — (*sighing*) Now I have to find a place where I can start a new life.

Tim — (*writing his home address down on a piece of paper*) Here...take this address and go live in my backyard. We are friendly to rabbits.

Mr. Rabbit ▶ (*tearful*) Really? Thank you so much! Now I owe you another favor.

Tim ▶ (*smiling*) Good luck!

第三幕

女士之夜

第一場

灰姑娘 ▶ 謝謝你們救了我，我可以為你們做什麼當作回報嗎？

提姆 ▶ （笑笑地）不用客氣。

巨人 ▶ 喔，或許你可以幫我？你知道如何讓我變回大巨人嗎？

灰姑娘 ▶ 對不起，我真的不知道…不過我認識的人當中可能有人知道！你要不要和我一起到我的讀書會再親自問她本人？

巨人 ▶ 真是太棒了！提姆，你回家前可以跟我們一起去嗎？

提姆 ▶ 當然可以！

灰姑娘 ▶ （感到沮喪）喔不！我藏在草叢裡時將火把熄滅了，沒辦法重新點燃！現在我無法辨識走到讀書會的秘密符號。

提姆	秘密符號看起來像什麼？

灰姑娘	我們總在沿途的樹上標記小小的 "R" 在樹上來帶路。

提姆	（從他的背包拿出手電筒）鏘鏘！提姆來拯救了！

巨人	哇！這火把很亮而且不燙耶。

提姆	你想要看更酷的東西嗎？ 提姆從背包拿出一個數位夜視雙筒望遠鏡，並秀給巨人看該如何使用。

巨人	酷哩！我剛剛看到那邊有鹿！

提姆	你可以幫我們注意危險的動物。 灰姑娘騎在馬上，提姆和巨人徒步走在前方帶路。走了一陣子之後，巨人忽然停住腳步並請他們安靜。

巨人	等等！（他拉著兔子先生的長耳朵，將他從草叢裡拉出來）啊！抓到了！看看我找到誰！

兔子先生	（踢著雙腳抗議中）放我下來！ 巨人放兔子下來。

提姆	又是你！你好啊！

兔子先生	（雙耳下垂）我比賽輸了！紅心皇后氣炸了！

灰姑娘	真是遺憾…不過試著保持樂觀！會有撥雲見日的時候！

兔子先生	（嘆口氣）現在我必須找個地方開始我的新生活。

提姆 ▶ （將他家地址寫在一張紙上）來…拿著這地址去我家後院生活，我們對兔子很友善的。

兔子先生 （含著淚）真的嗎？非常感謝你！我現在可是欠你兩份人情了。

提姆 ▶ （笑笑地）祝你好運！

Phrases & Sentence Patterns慣用語 & 句型

❶ in return 回報

❷ No worries. 不用客氣；小事一樁

❸ in person 親自；本人

❹ put out 撲滅

❺ to the rescue 來拯救

❻ watch out for somebody/something 留意；密切注意

❼ flip one's lid 暴怒（註：很像中文的「氣到頭頂冒煙」，想像水壺裡水煮滾時，蓋子噠噠噠作響的樣子，如同氣到頭頂蓋都掀起來了）

❽ Every cloud has a silver lining. 撥雲見日

The image of Cinderella is typically portrayed as innocent, kind, and beautiful. However, modern scriptwriters try to be playful and different. For example, in the movie Ella Enchanted (2004), starring Anna Hathaway, Ella is given the gift of obedience from an unreliable fairy named Lucinda. She must obey anything anyone tells her to do. The gift turns out to be a curse when her stepsisters use her obedience to get their way and tease her. Her obedience even nearly forces her to murder her love, Prince. Fortunately, Ella is able to use her willpower to defy the order and avoids crisis. In another movie titled Ever After: A Cinderella Story (2008), starring Drew Barrymore, Danielle is a Cinderella based character who is not very obedient, but still independent and smart like Ella. The protagonists in both movies guide their Prince to becoming good future kings. These characters fit the contemporary image of an independent and intelligent woman in mainstream Western culture.

文化角落

　　灰姑娘的典型形象一直是無辜、善良又美麗。然而，當代的編劇做了一些俏皮與不同的嘗試。舉例來說，電影《麻辣公主》（*Ella Enchanted*）（2004）中，女主角艾拉（*Ella*）（安海瑟薇 飾演）被不牢靠的仙女盧辛達（*Lucinda*）賜予「服從」這禮物，她必須服從任何人給她下的命令，當她的兩個繼姊利用她的順從來捉弄她時，這份禮物就變成一個詛咒。她的服從甚至害她差點被迫謀殺自己心愛的人，她的王子。所幸的是，艾拉有辦法以自己的意志力去抵抗命令，避免了一場危機。另一部電影《灰姑娘，很久很久以前》（*Ever After: A Cinderella Story*）（2008）中，女主角丹妮兒（*Danielle*）（朱爾巴蒂摩 飾演）也是依據灰姑娘這角色，只是不再像艾拉那樣順從，但一樣獨立又聰明。這兩部電影裡的女主角都引導她們的王子成為未來的好國王。這樣的角色符合現代西方主流社會裡，獨立又有智慧的女性形象。

Tim, the Giant, and Cinderella follow the 'R' symbols to the Princess Book Club, Cinderella introduces Tim and the Giant to her girls.

Tim   What's this Princess Book Club for?

Belle   I once found a book called *"Fairy Tales from the Brothers Grimm."* Part of the book was burned and all of the endings were tore off.

Cinderella   The weird thing was that many of the stories looked so familiar, so we decided to form a book club to discuss them.

Belle   Have you figured out the endings?

Cinderella   Not yet? But we have noticed a trend... the Queens and stepmothers don't treat their stepdaughters very well.

Belle   This book has helped us get through some difficult times. However, sometimes it's not easy to meet up. I am so happy that Cinderella was

able to make it this evening.

Tim ▸ I have an idea. My dad works at a technology company and is always bringing home electronic devices that have minor defects. I have quite a few handheld devices in my backpack I was supposed to bring to school for a charity sale.

Cinderella ▸ Uhhh....you're losing us.

Tim ▸ I just think I can help you keep in touch with each other more easily.

Tim hands each of them a device and helps them set up an account for a Social Networking app called Line.

Tim ▸ Surprising! The wireless connection is so good in this world! Now, if you can't meet up with each other, you can still have your book discussion in a chat room! As for charging your devices, use these portable chargers for now.

The girls are very excited to play with their new toys. Tim is so happy and proud that he is able to help the girls out.

Tim ▸ You can also take photos, record a voice message, or send emoticons to each other.

Cinderella ▸ I just sent a big smiley face to you. Do you see it yet, Swan Princess?

Swan Princess ▸ Where is it?

Tim ▸ (*pointing to her phone*) It's here!

Swan Princess ▸ Awesome! Let's see if I can send you a silly expression back.

Tim ▸ There you go! Good job, Swan Princess!

Swan Princess ▸ (*cheerfully*) Oh, I did it!

提姆、巨人和灰姑娘順著 R 符號的帶領來到公主們的讀書會。灰姑娘介紹提姆和巨人給她的姊妹淘認識。

提姆 ▸ 這公主讀書會的用意是什麼呢？

貝兒 ▸ 恩，我之前找到一本格林兄弟寫的書，叫做「童話故事」。書的一部份被燒毀了而且很多結局都被撕掉了。

灰姑娘 ▶ 奇怪的是，很多故事讀起來都很熟悉，所以我們決定成立一個讀書會來討論這些故事。

提姆 ▶ 你們討論出結局了嗎？

灰姑娘 ▶ 還沒？可是我們發現一個走向…皇后和後母都對她們的繼女都不是很好。

貝兒 ▶ 這本書幫助我們走過許多艱困的時候，不過有時候真的不容易聚在一起，我很高興灰姑娘今晚可以成功出席。

提姆 ▶ 我有個主意，我爸爸在一家科技公司上班，他總是會帶一些有些微瑕疵的電子設備回家，我背包裡有好一些掌上型電子設備，我本來是要帶去學校的慈善義賣會的。

灰姑娘 ▶ 恩…我們已經聽得一頭霧水了。

提姆 ▶ 我只是在想，我可以讓你們更容易聯絡上彼此。
提姆給她們一人一個設備並且幫她們在一個叫做 Line 的社群網絡設定好帳號。

提姆 ▶ 真是令人驚喜！這世界的無線收訊這麼好！現在，如果你們沒辦法碰面，可以在聊天室開讀書會！至於充電的問題，暫時先用這些攜帶式充電器吧。
女孩子們非常興奮地玩著新寵，提姆很高興也很驕傲自己可以幫得上忙。

提姆 ▶ 你也可以拍照，錄製語音訊息，或是傳情緒符號給對方。

灰姑娘 ▶ 我剛傳了一張大笑臉給你，白天鵝公主，你有看到嗎？

白天鵝公主 ▶ 在哪裡呢？

提姆 （指著她的手機）在這裡！

白天鵝公主 ▶ 好讚啊！讓我來試看看可不可以回傳一張搞笑的表情。

提姆 這就對了，你辦到了！很棒，白天鵝公主！

白天鵝公主 ▶ （雀躍地）喔，我會傳了！

Phrases & Sentence Patterns慣用語 & 句型

❶ get through some difficult times 度過艱難時刻

❷ meet up 碰頭；會面

❸ make it 成功；辦到

❹ You're losing us. 我們聽得一頭霧水了；我們聽不懂你在説什麼

❺ set up 設定

❻ as for 至於

❼ for now 暫時

❽ There you go. 這就對了，你成功做到了（在美式口語中，如果一個人正在嘗試某樣東西，最後終於成功了，在身旁的人，尤其是指導的人，可能會説 "There you go" 以表示肯定）

Cultural Note

The story of Beauty and the Beast is best known from Walt Disney's 1991 animation and the musical that played on Broadway from 1994 through 2007. However, the original fairy tale was much older than both these works! The story was written in the eighteenth century by French female author, Jeanne-Marie Le Prince de Beaumont! Now it makes more sense why the protagonist has a French name, Belle, which means "beauty" in French. The ending of the story implies that Belle is able to see the inner beauty of the Beast. Beauty and the Beast makes you wonder if fairy tales are teaching readers to appreciate people for who they truly are. However, not all the fairy tales tell the readers the same thing. You'd be surprised by the first version of the Frog Prince in Grimm's Fairy Tales. In the story, the princess takes the frog to her bedroom and becomes so angry that she throws the frog against the wall. Bang! The frog transforms into a handsome prince and the princess takes him as her companion. Ouch! That doesn't sound very romantic, does it?

　　迪士尼的動畫《美女與野獸》與百老匯上演的《美女與野獸》音樂劇（1994-2007）是最令一般人所熟知的。不過最初的童話故事比這兩部作品都來得老很多！法國女性作家 *Jeanne-Marie Le Prince de Beaumont* 在 18 世紀就寫了這故事！這樣一來，女主角的名字貝拉（*Belle*）源自法文，意思是「美女」，就很合理了！《美女與野獸》的結局暗示貝拉看到了野獸的內在美，讓人不禁猜想，童話故事是否是在教導讀者要懂得欣賞人的本質。不過，不是所有的童話故事都傳達同樣的道理。在格林童話最初版的《青蛙王子》故事中，公主將青蛙帶到她的臥房，但是她因為太生氣了就抓起青蛙往牆上摔過去。碰！青蛙變成一個英俊的王子，公主才接受他成為自己的人生伴侶！哎唷！聽起來就不是很浪漫，是不是呀？

 **Scene 3** ⭐ 🎧 MP3 13

Giant	Excuse me, does anyone know how to turn me back into a big giant?

The girls all shake their head.

Ariel	I wish I knew how to help you. Anyway, I met Thumbelina once. She told me that she hated being so small.

Tim	I thought Thumbelina was born small.

Ariel	She was, but it was because of a curse. She was back to her normal size after a true love's kiss. Unfortunately, when her husband died, she shrank again!

Tim	That's odd.

Ariel	When I met her, she said she found her second true love and her daughters, Anastasia and Drizella, were going to have a new father and a stepsister. She thought this true love's kiss

would change her back before the wedding but it didn't work.

Tim — Perhaps the fiancé is not her true love?

Ariel — I wonder that too.

Cinderella — Why do those names sound familiar? Oh, my God! Anastasia and Drizella are my stepsisters' names!

Tim — Thumbelina is your stepmother?

Cinderella — It all makes sense now! She wants EVERYTHING BIG! She loves big houses, big carts, big closets, big feet...

Everyone — Big feet?

Cinderella — Yes! No wonder she likes to tease me about my feet being so tiny and she is proud that Anastasia and Drizelle have bigger feet than mine.

Tim — Too big or not too big, that is the question.

Cinderella — It sure is.

Tim — Well, I have a feeling that your stepmother will be jealous of your tiny feet sooner or later!

Belle — (*to the Giant*) Well, it's pretty straightforward then. Just ask Cinderella's stepmother!

Cinderella — I am not so sure you want to mess with her.

Giant — No pain, no gain.

Cinderella — All right, as long as she does not freak out when she sees your small stature. By the way, she's meeting with her friends now. They always cast a magical spell around the area to keep people away so that no one can disturb them.

Tim — I have a jar of magic powder that I used to come here. It might be able to take me and The Giant to your stepmother. I'm going to give it a try.

Cinderella — Good luck!

第三場

巨人 ─ 不好意思，有人知道如何讓我變回大巨人嗎？
女孩們都搖頭。

艾瑞兒美人魚 ─ 但願我知道怎麼幫你，總之，我曾經碰過拇指姑娘，她跟我說很討厭自己這麼嬌小。

提姆 ─ 我以為拇指姑娘從出生就是很嬌小。

艾瑞兒美人魚 ─ 她是，不過是因為受詛咒，她在找到真愛之吻之後就變回原本的正常尺寸。不幸地是，當她先生過世時，她又再度縮小！

提姆 ─ 真是奇怪。

艾瑞兒美人魚 ─ 當我遇見她時，她說他已找到第二個真愛，她的女兒安娜塔西雅和德左拉很快就可以有個新爸爸和一個繼妹。她以為這個真愛之吻可以在婚禮之前讓她變回來，不過卻沒成功。

提姆 ─ 可能未婚夫不是她的真愛？

艾瑞兒美人魚 ─ 我也這麼想。

灰姑娘 ─ 為什麼那些名字這麼耳熟？喔，我的天啊！安娜塔西雅和德左拉是我繼姊的名字！

提姆 ─ 拇指姑娘是你的繼母？

灰姑娘 ▶ 一切都顯得非常合理了！她要每樣東西都很大！她喜歡大房子，大馬車，大衣櫥，大腳丫…

所有人 ▶ 大腳丫！？

灰姑娘 ▶ 是的！難怪她喜歡嘲笑我的腳很嬌小，還很自豪安娜塔西雅和德左拉的腳比我大。

提姆 ▶ 要不要與生俱有一雙大腳丫，還真是一個人生難題。

灰姑娘 ▶ 的確是這樣。

提姆 ▶ 恩，我有預感你的繼母不久就會羨慕你的小腳的。

貝兒 ▶ （對巨人說）那麼，答案顯而易見，你只要去問灰姑娘的繼母就行了！

灰姑娘 ▶ 我不確定你是否要去煩她。

巨人 ▶ 一分耕耘一分收穫，我總是要試看看。

灰姑娘 ▶ 好吧，只要她沒有因為看到你的小體型而抓狂。對了，她正在和朋友聚會，她們總是在周遭施魔法，讓其他人無法接近去打擾到他們。

提姆 ▶ 我這裡有一罐魔法粉末，當初就是用它才來到這裡的，或許它可以帶我和巨人到你繼母那裡，我要來試看看。

灰姑娘 ▶ 祝你們好運！

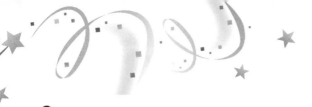

Phrases & Sentence Patterns慣用語 & 句型

❶ no wonder 難怪

❷ I wish I knew 但願我知道

❸ make sense 合理；說得通

❹ Too big or not too big, that's the question. 腳大腳小，這就是問題的所在。（此句改編自莎士比亞的悲劇「哈姆雷特」中著名獨白 "To be or not to be, that's the question." 如何詮釋與翻譯非一語能道盡故不在此討論，此名言句的結構也常用於節目中製造效／笑果。）

❺ sooner or later 遲早

❻ mess with someone 打擾（通常暗指對方不好惹，可能會惹麻煩上身）

❼ No pain, no gain. 一分耕耘一分收穫

❽ freak out （因為某事或某人）生氣；情緒或行為失控

Cultural Note

In Tokyo, where the population density is very high, tiny "capsule hotels" are popular for travelers and businessmen to spend their night in. These wouldn't go over well in the U.S. because many people embrace bigness. This concept is reflected in the huge food portions served by restaurants and many other things in American's lives. For example, unless you live in a big city like New York and

Act Three Scene 3

Chicago, many American's live in good sized homes with a front yard, a back yard, a garage, and a basement. Sometimes you can even see a gigantic truck transporting a pre-manufactured home on the highway. Sounds crazy? It's actually relatively common. However, there is a downside to owning a big home. It is easy for people to become hoarders with too many things stored in their basement and garage. At some point a garage sale is probably necessary to help empty some space and hope that their junk can become someone else's treasure!

文化角落

在東京這人口密度非常高的城市，小小的「膠囊旅館」很受到需要過夜的旅客和商務人士的青睞。然而，這種風格在美國就行不通，因為許多人擁抱「數大便是美」的概念，這概念反映在餐廳大份量的食物上，和其他美國生活方式。舉例來說，除非是住在像紐約和芝加哥那種大城市，許多美國人的家都有一定的規模，包括前院、後院、車庫和地下室。有時候你甚至可以看到巨大的卡車載著半成品的預售屋在高速公路上行走，聽起來很瘋狂？但實際上還挺普遍的。不過，擁有一間大房子有一個缺點，那就是，很容易囤積物品在地下室和車庫。到了一定程度，車庫拍賣或許就變成必要的手段，來騰出一些空間，同時期望自己用不到的東西可以變成別人的寶貝！

As the Wizard promises, the 'Essence of Rainbow' magical powder does help Tim to travel within the World of Wonderland. After flying through the sky for a while, Tim and the Giant fall down into a field. In a distance, they see a group of people gathered around a bonfire. Tim and the Giant approach and hide behind a big tree.

The Queen — Snow White has had a really short fuse recently. She's broken several magical mirrors and even cut down my apple trees.

Cinderella's Stepmother — It's better than seeing Cinderella's small feet every day.

The Queen — What's wrong with small feet?

Cinderella's Stepmother — EVERYTHING is wrong when it's SMALL!

The Queen — My dear, you really have an issue!

Cinderella's Stepmother — Yeah yeah, you talk as if you are not obsessed with your magical mirror.

Act Three Scene 4

The Queen — (*laughing widely*) You're right. I have to say, being a stepmom is never an easy task, not to mention dealing with young girls.

Cinderella's Stepmother — I second that.

The Queen — Fortunately, I have something else to entertain me now.

The Queen shows the group her edited photos she made using the app Tim gave her.

Cinderella's Stepmother — Look at that smooth skin on your face. Your double chin is gone!! I bet looking at that photo can help you sweep all your worries under the rug.

The Queen — Yes, at least temporarily. Actually, with these photos, I am starting a new life... (*She lowers her voice.*) I have signed up for online dating.

Cinderella's Stepmother — What's that? What did you say?

The Queen — Hmm... I don't know how to explain.

Tim — (*jumping suddenly out from behind the tree*) Please, allow me to explain. Online dating is where you meet people in a virtual world. You chat with each other online first before you really see them in person.

第四場

　　如同巫師所承諾的，彩虹元素魔法粉末的確幫助提姆在魔幻世界中穿梭。提姆和巨人在天空飛了一陣子之後，掉落到一個平原上。 他們看到一群人正在遠處圍著營火。提姆和巨人靠近她們，並躲在一棵大樹後面。

皇后 — 白雪公主最近的脾氣非常不好，她打破好幾個魔鏡，甚至砍倒我的蘋果樹。

灰姑娘的繼母 — 總比我每天都要見到灰姑娘的小腳來得好。

皇后 — 小腳有什麼問題嗎？

灰姑娘的繼母 — 只要是小尺寸的東西就是不對勁！

皇后 — 親愛的，你的想法實在有點問題！

灰姑娘的繼母 — 是啦是啦，你説得像是你自己完全沒有對魔鏡過度著迷。

皇后 — （狂笑）也是。我必須説，當後母還真不是一件簡單的任務，更不用説還得應付年輕女孩了。

灰姑娘的繼母 ▶ 我完全同意。

皇后 ▶ 幸好我現在有別的東西可以讓我開心。
皇后秀給大家看她用提姆所給的應用程式所編輯的照片。

灰姑娘的繼母 ▶ 瞧你臉上的光滑肌膚，你的雙下巴也不見了！！我敢說看
了這些照片之後能讓你一掃所有的擔憂。

皇后 ▶ 是的，至少可以暫時忘掉煩惱。其實我還用這些照片開啟
了新的人生…（她壓低聲音）我加入一個線上約會網站。

灰姑娘的繼母 ▶ 那是什麼？你說什麼？

皇后 ▶ 恩…我也不知道該怎麼解釋。

提姆 ▶ （忽然從樹後跳出來）請容許我來解釋。線上約會就是在
虛擬的世界認識別人，在你見到對方本尊之前，一開始可
以先在線上聊天。

Phrases & Sentence Patterns慣用語 & 句型

❶ have a short fuse 脾氣不好；易怒

❷ be obsessed with 著迷於…

❸ not to mention someone/something 更不用提…

❹ I second that. 我贊同／支持

❺ weep all your worries under the rug 一掃所有的擔憂

❻ sign up for 參加

❼ online dating 線上交友

❽ Please allow me to +V.（客氣用法）請容許我...

Cultural Note

In the U.S. Midwest, family and friends enjoy getting together on nice fall evenings to relax and converse while sitting around a gentle bonfire. While enjoying a cold beer, people also like to cook foods above the bonfire, such as hotdogs and S'mores. A very long fork-like tool (commonly called a hotdog fork) allows you to hold hotdogs above the fire without burning yourself. After enjoying some hotdogs and beer, making some "S'mores" is an entertaining and fun dessert. First, put a couple marshmallows on the two ends of a fork first and hold them above the fire. You must rotate the hotdog fork constantly, so the surface of the marshmallows turns a little brown. However, you must be careful not to let the marshmallows get too soft or they'll slide off the fork and into the bonfire! Once they're done, quickly grab two pieces of Graham Crackers sandwich your marshmallows with a piece of chocolate in between. Then simply take a bite and enjoy your S'mores!

文化角落

　　在美國的中西部，家人和朋友很喜歡在清朗的秋夜聚在一起，圍坐在溫暖的營火前面放鬆聊天。一邊享受冰冰的啤酒的同時，也喜歡邊在營火上面烤東西，像是熱狗或棉花糖餅乾三明治（S'mores）。有一種長長像叉子一樣的工具（一般稱為熱狗叉）讓你可以將熱狗放在營火上頭卻又不會燙到自己。享用完一些熱狗和啤酒之後，烤棉花糖餅乾三明治（S'mores）是好玩又具有娛樂效果的點心。首先，將兩個棉花糖放在叉子的兩端，並放在營火上烤，你必須持續地轉動熱狗叉，烤到棉花糖的表面有點變得焦焦的，不過又必須很小心才不會讓棉花糖變得太軟，否則就會滑落叉子，掉到營火裡！烤好之後，必須快速地拿兩片全麥餅乾（Graham crackers），將棉花糖和一塊巧克力夾在其中。再來就是直接咬上一口，好好享受你的棉花糖餅乾三明治囉！

The Queen	(*clapping*) Well said, Tim!

Tim	Thank you, Your Majesty.

The Queen	Actually, I've already made plans to meet up with this guy I've been chatting with for a while.

Tim	Good for you.

The Queen	By the way, what on earth are you doing here? I thought you were sent home.

Giant	I asked him to join me. I am looking for Thumbelina.

Suddenly the bonfire disappears. The face of Cinderella's Stepmother turns red with anger.

Cinderella's Stepmother	How dare you mention that name here?

Giant	I... .I... I just want to know how to undo the magic that turned me into a dwarf.

Act **Three** Scene 5

Tim　Please, forgive my friend's abruptness. Would you try to help him?

The Queen　I think you guys had better leave before it's too late.

Cinderella's Stepmother　I will give you a chance to save yourself from certain death by telling me who spilled the beans and guided you here.

Tim　(*trying not to cause Cinderella trouble*) Ah... hmmm... Hans Anderson!

Everyone　Who's Hans Anderson?

Tim　He is the greatest wizard in the world. He can look into the past and foretell the future.

The Queen　Really? Will I always be the fairest of all in this world?

Tim　Well, now that you have the app. You are the fairest of all in the virtual world. Keep up the good work.

Cinderella's Stepmother Did this great wizard foresee the fate that lies ahead for you?

Tim No, ma'am.

Cinderella's Stepmother Let me be your prophet. You both will be turned into rocks with big heads.

Giant Oh, no. A dwarf with a big head is not very well proportioned, not attractive at all.

Tim No thanks. My parents always taught me to be humble.

Cinderella's Stepmother No worries. I will make you a proud big-headed ROCK.

Tim I'm sorry but, with all due respect, this trick is lame. Mr. Anderson, the greatest wizard, already showed it to me.

Cinderella's Stepmother No way. This is one of my specialties.

Tim I'll show you proof.

皇后	（拍拍手）提姆，說得很好！
提姆	謝謝皇后陛下！
皇后	其實，我已經計畫好要和聊了一陣子天的一個男士見面。
提姆	很好唷！
皇后	對了，你怎麼會跑到這裡來？我以為我已經送你回家了。
巨人	是我要他跟我一起來的，我正在尋找拇指姑娘。 忽然營火消失了，灰姑娘的繼母整張臉因為生氣而漲紅。
灰姑娘的繼母	你竟敢在這裡提起那名字？
巨人	我…我…我只是想要知道如何解除使我變成小矮人的魔法。
提姆	拜託，請原諒我朋友魯莽的行為，您可以幫幫他嗎？
皇后	我想趁現在還來得及，你們最好離開。
灰姑娘的繼母	我讓你們有一次機會免死，只要告訴我是誰洩密引你們到這裡找我。
提姆	（努力不造成灰姑娘的麻煩）啊…恩…是漢斯安徒生！

所有人 ▶ 誰是漢斯安徒生？

提姆 ▶ 他是全世界最偉大的巫師，他可以一探過去也可以預知未來。

皇后 ▶ 真的嗎？那我會不會一直是這世界最美的一位？

提姆 ▶ 這個嘛，你現在有了這應用程式，是虛擬世界裡最美的一位，繼續保持努力 。

灰姑娘的繼母 ▶ 這位偉大的巫師有沒有預言你眼前的命運呢？

提姆 ▶ 沒有，夫人。

灰姑娘的繼母 ▶ 讓我來當你們的預言家，你們將會變成兩個頭很大的石頭（big head 暗指自大）。

巨人 ▶ 喔不要，小矮人配上大頭不是很好的身材比例，一點都不迷人。

提姆 ▶ 喔，不用麻煩了，謝謝。我的父母一直教導我做人要謙虛。

灰姑娘的繼母 ▶ 別擔心，我會讓你們成為驕傲又自大的大頭石。

提姆 ▶ 不好意思，不過恕我直言，這把戲太弱了， 因為安徒生先生已經秀給我看過了。

灰姑娘的繼母 ▶ 不可能的，這可是我的拿手絕活之一。

 提姆 ▶ 我給你看證據。

Phrases & Sentence Patterns慣用語 & 句型

❶ Good for you！（用來肯定對方的成功或是好運氣）幹得好！真棒！太幸運了！

❷ on earth 究竟

❸ How dare you…膽敢；斗膽

❹ had better + 原形動詞：最好…

❺ spill the beans 洩密

❻ Keep up the good work！（鼓勵對方）繼續努力保持（好表現之類的）

❼ big-headed 自負的；傲慢的

❽ with all due respect 恕我直言；無意冒犯；冒昧說一句（通常是下對上時，或要反對別人意見時所說的客氣話當開場白）

Besides the Brothers Grimm, Hans Anderson also created numerous well-known characters in his fairy tales, such as The Little Mermaid, The Ugly Duckling, The Snow Queen, The Emperor's Clothes, and Thumbelina. Thumbelina is a story of a little girl no more than a thumb-joint high. One night she is taken by the mother toad, who plans for her to marry her son. After escaping from the toads, she meets other animals. Whereas some try to set her up for a marriage, others help her to escape. Eventually, she meets the flower-fairy prince who is just as petite as she is. Interestingly, a recurring theme throughout the story is the idea of an "arranged marriage" and how the little girl avoids being set up. Nowadays, most American's enjoy the freedom to choose their life partner, but some still struggle to escape from family/societal pressures. From this perspective, Thumbelina, written in the nineteenth century, discusses an issue that still exists in some corners of the world.

文化角落

　　除了格林兄弟（*Brothers Grimm*）之外，漢斯安徒生（*Hans Anderson*）也在他的童話故事裡，創造了無數知名的角色，像是《小美人魚》、《醜小鴨》、《雪王后》、《國王的新衣》和《拇指姑娘》。《拇指姑娘》敘述一個不到一個拇指大的小女孩的故事，有一天晚上她被母癩蛤蟆帶走，計畫將她嫁給自己的兒子。在順利逃脫癩蛤蟆之後，她遇到其他動物，有些試圖幫她安排婚姻大事，有些則幫助她逃脫。最後她遇見花之精靈王子，個頭就和她一樣嬌小。有趣的是，整個故事有一個不斷重複的主題，就是「被安排好的婚姻」（*arranged marriage*），以及這小女孩如何一再避免被撮合。如今，很多美國人都享受自由選擇伴侶的權利，但有一些人依舊努力要逃離家庭或社會的壓力。從這角度來看，在 19 世紀出版的《拇指姑娘》，其所探討的議題至今依舊存在於世界上一些角落的。

Tim pulls out his iPad and shows the ladies a picture of Mount Rushmore.

Cinderella's Stepmother — No, it can't be!

Giant — Guess somebody needs to learn a new trick.

Cinderella's Stepmother — Watch your tongue, dwarf. Or I will remove it from your mouth

Giant — (*covering his mouth with both hands*) Yes, ma'am.

The Queen — Sorry, sister, but these rock heads look magnificent. And I must say, these gentlemen are very handsome! I wonder if they would care to try an online date?

Tim — Aaah... Your Majesty, I think they prefer to write letters.

The Queen — What a shame!

Cinderella's Stepmother Kid, I will spare your life, but only if you hook me up with Mr. Anderson.

Tim Hmm... .I think he's currently out traveling around for his 'Wizard-Wicked-Woohoo workshops'.

Cinderella's Stepmother Then I guess I have no choice but to turn you into a rock. Perhaps Mr. Anderson will come to me eventually.

Tim Wait, it just occurred to me that Mr. Anderson is currently in Denmark. If you tell The Giant how to undo the magic spell and let us go, I will contact him right away.

Cinderella's Stepmother You've got yourself a deal.

Tim starts writing an email to his language arts teacher, Mr. Anderson, whose last name is the same as the great fairy tale author Hans Anderson. Mr. Anderson requires each of his students to write a story for him during the summer.
The email said:
Dear Mr. Anderson,
How are you? As you mentioned earlier, the power of mind is magical

and the power of art can turn an ordinary rock into a masterpiece. However, in pursuit of the task, I find myself stuck in my fairytale world. Can you reveal your secret for turning a rock into a work of art and save me from my misery?

Sincerely,

Tim BeauDaring

Tim ─ Ok, the message has been sent.

Cinderella's Stepmother ─ Very well. You will be held as my prisoners until we hear back from him. Here, have some S'mores.

提姆拿出他的 iPad 給女士們看一張拉什莫爾山（Mount Rushmore) 的照片。

灰姑娘的繼母 ─ 不，不可能的！

巨人 ─ 我猜有人需要學新把戲了。

灰姑娘的繼母 ─ 説話給我小心點，小矮人，否則我就割掉你嘴巴裡的舌頭。

巨人 ─ （用雙手遮住他的嘴巴）是的，夫人。

皇后 ─ 真是抱歉，好姊妹，但這些石頭像看起來真的很壯觀，而

且我必須說，這幾位男士很英俊！我在想，他們願意嘗試線上約會嗎？

提姆 ▶ 啊⋯殿下我想他們比較喜歡寫書信。

皇后 ▶ 太可惜了！

灰姑娘的繼母 ▶ 小子，我可以饒你一命，不過條件是你要安排我認識安徒生先生。

提姆 ▶ 恩⋯我想他目前正因為他的「巫師怪怪唷呼座談會」到處旅行當中。

灰姑娘的繼母 ▶ 那麼，我別無選擇只能將你變成一顆石頭，然後，或許安徒生先生最後會來我這裡找你。

提姆 ▶ 等等，我忽然想到安徒生先生目前正在丹麥，如果你告訴巨人如何解除魔法並且放我們走的話，我可以立刻聯絡他。

灰姑娘的繼母 ▶ 就照你說的做。

　　提姆開始寫信給他的語文學老師，安徒生先生，他的姓氏剛剛好與偉大的童話故事作家漢斯安徒生一樣，安徒生先生要求每一位學生在暑假期間寫一篇故事給他。

電子郵件寫道：

親愛的安徒生先生：

　　你好嗎？如你先前提及的，心靈的力量如魔法，藝術的力量可以點石成曠世傑作。然而，在追求這任務的過程中，我發現自己困在自己的童話故事裡。你可以透露如何點石成極品的方法，將我從不幸當中解救出來嗎？

提姆博德林　敬上

 提姆　　好了，訊息已送出去了。

灰姑娘的繼母　　很好，在收到他的回信前，你就一直是我的囚犯，來，吃些烤棉花糖餅乾三明治（S'mores）。

Phrases & Sentence Patterns慣用語 & 句型

❶ It can't be！（通常使用在對某事難以置信時）不可能的！

❷ learn a new trick 學新把戲（源自 "You can't teach an old dog new tricks." 老狗玩不出新把戲。）

❸ Watch you tongue. 説話給我小心點

❹ care to do something 願意做某事；想做某事

❺ What a shame！太可惜了！

❻ only if 唯有（在某種條件之下）…

❼ hook someone up（with someone）安排與誰見面或共事

❽ It just occurred to someone that 忽然想到

Cultural Note

Mount Rushmore, one of America's famous tourist locations, is located in South Dakota's Black Hills National Forest. Mount Rushmore symbolizes freedom and hope for America. The southeast side of the mountain has four gigantic carved sculptures, which are the faces of U.S. Presidents George Washington, Thomas Jefferson, Abraham Lincoln, and Theodore Roosevelt. It took the sculptor, Gutzon Borglum, and his team over a decade (from 1927-1941) to complete the project. Seeing the sculptures in person will leave you in awe of the incredible hand-made artwork blending with the beauty of nature. Besides Mount Rushmore, there are numerous other activities to enjoy in Black Hills National Forest, such as picnicking, camping, climbing, fishing, and horseback riding. The beauty of nature will not fail you, if you ever decide to spend a couple of nights here. By the way, be sure to bring some warm clothes, as it can be chilly during the night.

　　位於南達科他州（South Dakota）黑崗國家森林公園（Black Hills National Forest）的拉什莫爾山（Mount Rushmore）是美國著名的觀光景點之一，對美國而言，拉什莫爾山（Mount Rushmore）象徵著自由與希望。山的東南邊有四座巨大雕像，分別是華盛頓（George Washington）、傑佛遜（Thomas Jefferson）、林肯（Abraham Lincoln）和羅斯福（Theodore Roosevelt）。雕刻家 Gutzon Borglum 和他的團隊前後花了將近 12 年的時間（1927-1941）才完成這工程。親眼見到雕像時，會讓你讚歎這不可思議的手雕藝術是如何的與自然美景融為一體。除了拉什莫爾山（Mount Rushmore）之外，還可以在 黑崗國家森林公園（Black Hills National Forest）從事許多其他活動，像是野餐、露營、攀岩、釣魚和騎馬。如果決定在這待上一兩晚的話，自然美景絕對不會讓你失望的。對了，一定要記得帶些保暖衣物，因為入夜之後可是會有點冷的。

Back to Where It Started

Dairy Queen	(*pointing at Tim's iPad*) Excuse me. I just noticed a big sign with my name showing on your magical box.

Tim	That's an advertisement for Dairy Queen.

Dairy Queen	But I am The Dairy Queen, mother of dairy products.

Tim	Cool. I've always loved the ice cream at Dairy Queen.

Dairy Queen	Ice cream? Great idea for my next party. I can ask the Snow Queen to freeze some of my cream into ice cream. Hmm··· milk might be even better. Then I can pour some hot chocolate syrup on top of the frozen milk for a perfect combination. And then I can squeeze

some whipped cream on top. Yum! I'm so talented!

Tim → You can even sprinkle some chocolate chips on top.

Dairy Queen → What a wonderful idea! Ok, you're invited!

Tim → Thank you! I'd love to go.

Giant → You guys need to stay on topic. (*To Cinderella's Stepmom.*) Let's not beat around the bush. Are you able to teach me how to reverse the magic spell now or not?

Cinderella's Stepmother → That's easy. Just eat the right breakfast and you will grow up in no time!

Tim & Giant → The right breakfast?

Cinderella's Stepmother → One night, when I was in despair, the Witch of the Candy House invited me to her place to comfort me. The next morning she made me a very delicious breakfast. The more I ate, the bigger I got. Eventually, I grew to a normal size.

Giant ▶ You're making all this up. We already talked to the Witch, and she doesn't know how to turn me back.

Cinderella's Stepmother ▶ It's up to you if you want to believe me or not. The previous witch that I met passed all her powers to the current witch, who happens to be awfully forgetful. Just ask for her famous King's Pancakes and make sure you remind her to follow the recipe.

第三幕

回到最初的起點

冰雪皇后 ▶ （指著提姆的 iPad）不好意思，我注意到你這神奇的盒子裡有個大大的牌子寫著我的名字。

提姆 ▶ 那是冰雪皇后的廣告。

冰雪皇后 ▶ 可是我就是冰雪皇后，乳製品之母。

提姆 ▶ 酷耶，我一直很喜歡冰雪皇后這牌子的冰淇淋。

冰雪皇后　▶　冰淇淋？太棒的主意了，可以用在下一次的派對上，我可以請冰雪女王冷凍一些鮮奶油讓它變成冰淇淋。恩…等等，我覺得冷凍牛奶甚至更好，然後我可以倒一些熱巧克力糖漿在冷凍牛奶上面，這將會是完美的組合，然後我還可以擠一些鮮奶油在上面。太可口了！我真是天才！

提姆　▶　你甚至可以灑一些巧克力碎片在上面。

冰雪皇后　▶　真是好主意！你已被邀請到我下一個派對了！

提姆　▶　謝謝！我很樂意參加。

巨人　▶　你們不要岔開主題。（對灰姑娘的繼母説）我們就別再拐彎抹角了，您可以教教我翻轉魔法的方法嗎？

灰姑娘的繼母　▶　很簡單啊。只要你吃對早餐，你就會立刻長大！

提姆&巨人　▶　吃對早餐？

灰姑娘的繼母　▶　有一晚，當我感到絕望時，糖果屋的巫婆邀我進去她家並安慰我，隔天早晨，她做了一個非常美味的早餐，我吃越多就長越大，最後我就長回原本的尺寸。

巨人　▶　您亂掰故事的吧，我們已經和糖果屋的巫婆談過，她不知道如何將我變回來。

灰姑娘的繼母　▶　信不信由你，我碰到的是上任的糖果屋巫婆，她將魔法力都傳給現任這一位顯然非常健忘的巫婆，你只要請她做國王鬆餅，並且務必提醒她照著食譜做就行了。

Phrases & Sentence Patterns慣用語 & 句型

❶ Stay on topic. 不要岔開主題

❷ Beat around the bush.拐彎抹角

❸ in no time 立刻；馬上

❹ in despair 絕望地

❺ The more 主詞 1+動詞 1, the 形容詞比較級 + 主詞 2+ 動詞 2: 主詞 1 越…,主詞 2 就越…

❻ make something up 編造；捏造

❼ It's up to you. 由你決定

❽ happen to + 原型動詞：碰巧

Cultural Note

Dairy Queen is a chain restaurant primarily founded in the U.S., but has expanded its business internationally and its ice-cream treats are now known throughout the world. One thing unique about Dairy Queen in the U.S. is the stores usually have a parking lot as well as outdoor benches and tables for customers. The idea is very simple - ice cream melts fast, so one must enjoy it right away! Therefore, people usually enjoy their ice cream while sitting in their cars or on a bench. Families have enjoyed ice cream this way for generations. Grandpa and grandson create lasting memories *bonding while having a waffle cone full of ice cream sitting in the car on a hot summer day. Today people in Taiwan can try Dairy Queen ice cream as well. Unfortunately, the stores are all located inside a department store. Next time, when you have an ice cream treat, just close your eyes and imagine that you're eating it in a car while enjoying the summer breeze!*

文化角落

　　冰雪皇后（Dairy Queen）是一家連鎖餐廳，創建於美國但在透過國際化經營之後，該品牌的冰淇淋已是全世界知曉的。美國的冰雪皇后（Dairy Queen）很獨特的地方是，店家通常會有一個停車場以及戶外的長凳和桌子供顧客使用。理由很簡單，冰淇淋融得快，一拿到手就要立刻享受！因此，人們常常坐在車子內或是長凳上享受他們的冰淇淋。許多家庭一代代這樣吃著冰淇淋，炎炎夏日時，當爺爺和孫子一起坐在車內享受冰淇淋甜筒時，他們便一起創造了深刻的情感記憶連結。現在在台灣也可以品嚐到冰雪皇后冰淇淋，可惜的是，店家都位於百貨公司裡。下一次當你吃著冰淇淋美食時，閉上眼睛，想像自己一邊享受著夏日微風，一邊坐在車裡吃著冰淇淋！

| Tim | Oh look, I just received Mr. Anderson's reply. |

Dear Tim,

I'm pleased to hear from you. I've noticed that you're having a very productive summer. As to your question, there aren't really any rules for turning rock into a work of art. Just follow your heart and look for something extraordinary out of the ordinary. When necessary, revise until it feels right.

Enjoy your magic-making adventure!

Best wishes,

Mr. Andersen

| Cinderella's Stepmother | Hmmm... revise until it feels right? (*She announces out of the blue.*) Okay. Let me turn you into a rock with this version of the spell. |

| Tim & Giant | What? |

| The Queen | Sister, not so fast! My app has a glitch. I need Tim to fix it for me. |

| Dairy Queen | Yeah. Don't be so hasty. I am wondering |

whether the Dairy Queen on his magical box could be a clue about my lost twin sister?

Cinderella's Stepmother — I have just had an inspiration!

Giant — (*shouting nervously*) Tim! You've got to do something!

Tim hastily rummages through his backpack and grabs the first thing he can get his hands on.

Tim — (*shouting out loud as if he were Doreamon*) Look, it's a remote control!

Cinderella's Stepmother — A remote control? Don't worry, I won't be casting you off to a remote place. You will be sitting RIGHT HERE as hard as a rock.

Cinderella's Stepmother starts speaking in gibberish and is about to cast her spell. Tim is so nervous that he clutches the remote control tightly in both hands like a defensive weapon. He closes his eyes and instinctively points the remote control toward Cinderella's Stepmother and accidently pushes the pause button. She suddenly stops speaking. Tim realizes that everyone in front of him is frozen, with exception of the Giant who happens to be hiding behind him. Astonished at the turn of events, Tim uses some of the 'Essence of Rainbow' magic powder to get the Giant and himself out of there immediately.

第二場

提姆 ── 你們瞧，我剛收到安徒生先生的回信。

親愛的提姆：
很高興收到你的消息，我有注意到你的夏天非常有收穫，有關你的問題，想要「點石成極品」並沒有真正的規則，只要跟著你的心走，從平凡的事物當中找出特別的點，必要時，修改它直到滿意為止。
好好享受製造魔法的冒險！
最誠摯的祝福，
安徒生先生

灰姑娘的繼母 ── 恩…修改它直到滿意為止？（她出乎意料地宣布）好吧，讓我用這版本的咒語將你們變成石頭看看。

提姆&巨人 ── 啥！？

皇后 ── 好姊妹，別急啊！我的應用程式有小狀況，我需要提姆幫我修一下。

冰雪皇后 ── 對啊，別急別急，我也正好奇，他魔法箱裡的那個冰雪皇后是不是可以提供關於我失散已久的雙胞胎妹妹的線索。

Act Four Scene 2

灰姑娘的繼母　　我正好有個靈感！很可能隨時都會不見，所以我現在就要試看看。

巨人　　（緊張地大叫）提姆！你得想想辦法啊！
提姆倉促地在背包裡亂搜，拿起手裡可抓到的第一件物品。

提姆　　（大叫出來彷彿自己是哆啦 A 夢）你們瞧，是一個遙控器！

灰姑娘的繼母　　遙控器？別擔心，我不會將你們丟到遙遠的地方去，你們會牢牢地像石頭般穩固的豎立在此。

　　灰姑娘的繼母開始說一些令人聽不懂的話，準備要下她的咒語。提姆因為很緊張就用雙手上緊緊抓住遙控器，像是握著防衛性武器一樣，他閉上眼睛很本能地將遙控器指向灰姑娘的繼母並不小心地按下了暫停鍵，灰姑娘的繼母忽然沒講話了。提姆發現，除了剛好躲在他背後的巨人之外，他眼前的人都暫停不動了，雖然對事情的轉折感到驚訝，提姆立刻使用彩虹元素魔法粉末，帶著巨人逃離現場。

Phrases & Sentence Patterns慣用語 & 句型

❶ as to 至於；關於
❷ when necessary 必要時
❸ out of the blue 出乎意料地
❹ wonder whether 想知道；（正式和禮貌上的請求）不知能否…

❺ as adj. as + 名詞 如…一樣的

❻ in gibberish 説的話像是胡言亂語，讓人聽不懂

❼ so…that 因為…就；因為…以至於

❽ with exception of 除了…之外

Cultural Note

In the U.S. if you want to start your weekend with home-make pancakes, the easiest way is to use a box of pancake mix. Then, all you have to do is to stir the mixture with eggs, milk, and a little oil. If you want to make pancake from scratch, here is an easy recipe for you!

Ingredients: 1 ½ all-purpose flour, 3 ½ teaspoons baking powder, 1 teaspoon salt, 1 table spoon white sugar, 1 ¼ cups milk, 1 egg, 3 tablespoons melted butter

Directions:

1. In a large bowl, stir the flour, baking powder, salt and sugar together and then make a well in the center to pour in milk, egg and melted butter.

2. Stir everything until just moistened (do not over mix, there should be a few lumps).

3. Pour a little olive oil onto a frying pan and heat it on a medium setting. Spoon the batter into the pan and use the back of the spoon to spread

batter into a round.

4. Once the air bubbles on top of the pancake have popped, you're ready to flip your pancake over to brown the other side. Serve immediately with warmed maple syrup or other desired toppings.

文化角落

　　在美國，如果你想要以自製的鬆餅展開週末，最容易的方式就是使用一盒預先調配好的鬆餅粉。然後，你只需要將鬆餅粉和蛋、牛奶和少許油混合在一起即可。如果你想要從頭開始做鬆餅，這裡有個很簡單的食譜！

　　材料：1½ 杯中筋麵粉、3½ 茶匙泡打粉、1 茶匙鹽、1 大匙白色砂糖、1¼ 杯 牛奶、1 顆蛋、3 大匙 軟化的奶油步驟：

　　1 在一個大碗裡將麵粉、泡打粉、鹽巴和糖攪拌均勻之後，在中間挖一個井般的凹洞，再倒進牛奶、蛋和軟化的奶油。

　　2 將所有東西攪拌在一起直到材料混合成黏稠狀，但不要過度攪拌，應該要看得到一點麵糰塊。

　　3 到一點橄欖油到平底鍋裡，以中火加熱。舀一湯匙麵糊到平底鍋，用湯匙背面將麵糊整型成圓形。

　　4 當鬆餅上面出現氣泡時，就可以翻面，直到另一面也煎到變棕色，然後立刻裝盤並淋上加熱後的楓糖漿或是其他你想要的配料。

After being carried around in the wind for a while, Tim and the Giant fall onto the dining table in the Candy House. The Witch of the Candy House, Hansel and Gretel are just about to eat.

Witch	(*startled*) Oh! Look who's joined us for dinner! What a feast!
Giant	(*pointing at Tim*) He's a real boy, much more delicious than me.
Tim	(*mockingly*) What a good friend!
Witch	(*holding up her folk and knife*) Young kids make my mouth water. Hansel and Gretel, should we grill him or boil him?
Hansel & Gretel	(*chuckling*) BOTH!
Tim	I am poisonous! If you come one step closer you'll regret it!
Witch	(*laughing wildly*) No worries, kiddo. We're just

Act Four Scene 3

joking. We don't eat kids. I'm a vegetarian.

Tim & Giant — What? But people always warn kids to stay away from you.

Witch — The old witch living in this house did enjoy the flesh of children. After she passed this house on to me, I found it entertaining to keep up her reputation.

Tim — What a relief!

Witch — Now tell us what brings you here on top of our dining table?

Tim & Giant — (*climbing off the dining table*) Oh, we're so sorry.

Giant — Cinderella's Stepmother told us that your King's Pancakes could change me back.

Witch — Oh yeah, you're right! I almost forget that the recipe has magical power.

The Witch gets up from the table and starts to search through her

kitchen cabinets for the recipe.

Witch — (*reading the recipe*) This pancake needs very special ingredients. The Wizard's magical flour, cow milk from the Dairy Queen, the Giant's golden eggs, and maple syrup from the Queen of Hearts. I'm afraid that I have let you down because I don't have all the ingredients.

Giant — No problem! Keep those eggs I gave you earlier and we'll get the rest.

Witch — Ooops. We ate them all! That runny yolk went so well with toast.

Giant — What? I shouldn't have put all my golden eggs into one basket. It will take me forever to climb up the beanstalk and get more.

Tim — Easy come, easy go.

第三場

隨風飄動了好一陣子，提姆和巨人掉落在糖果屋的餐桌上，糖果屋的巫婆，漢賽爾和葛麗特正打算開動吃飯。

巫婆 （嚇到）看看誰來晚餐了！真是美食當前！

巨人 （指著提姆）他是真男孩，吃起來比我可口。

提姆 （語帶嘲諷地說）你還真是好朋友啊！

巫婆 （拿起她的刀叉）幼嫩的小孩讓我口水直流，漢賽爾和葛麗特，我們應該烤他還是水煮呢？

漢賽爾和葛麗特 （呵呵地笑）兩種口味都要！

提姆 我有毒！如果你們再靠近一步的話，會後悔的！

巫婆 （狂笑）別擔心，小子，我們只是在開玩笑，我們不吃小孩的，我吃素。

提姆&巨人 什麼！？可是大家總是警告小孩別靠近你。

巫婆 之前住在這裡的老巫婆的確喜歡吃小孩的肉，當她將房子交給我時，我覺得保留她這名聲還挺有趣的。

提姆 真是令人鬆一口氣！

| 巫婆 | 現在快告訴我，是什麼風把你們吹到我的餐桌上？ |

| 提姆&巨人 | （從餐桌上爬下來）喔，真對不起。 |

| 巨人 | 灰姑娘的繼母告訴我們，你的國王鬆餅可以將我變回來。 |

| 巫婆 | 喔是的，你說對了！我差點忘記那食譜有魔法的力量。
巫婆從餐桌上起身，開始在她廚房的櫥櫃尋找食譜。 |

| 巫婆 | （讀著食譜）這鬆餅需要非常特別的材料：巫師的魔法麵粉，冰雪皇后的牛奶，巨人的金雞蛋，和紅心皇后的楓糖漿。看來恐怕要讓你失望了，因為我沒有所有的材料。 |

| 巨人 | 沒問題，你留著我之前給你的金雞蛋，我們會找到其他的材料。 |

| 巫婆 | 阿喔，都吃完了！蛋黃液和吐司真是絕配。 |

| 巨人 | 什麼！？我實在不應該將我的金雞蛋都放在同一個籃子裡，我現在大概要花一輩子的時間才能爬上豌豆去拿更多金雞蛋。 |

| 提姆 | 真是來得快，去得也快呀！ |

Phrases & Sentence Patterns慣用語 & 句型

❶ What a feast. 真是一頓饗宴
❷ make one's mouth water 垂延三尺
❸ What a relief！鬆一口氣了
❹ What brings you 什麼原因讓你前來

❺ let someone down 使某人失望

❻ something goes well with 搭配；適合

❼ have put all my golden eggs into your basket，改編自 "put all your eggs into one basket" 將雞蛋放在同一個籃子，暗喻沒有分散風險

❽ Easy come, easy go. 來得快，去得也快

Cultural Note

　　Giving a compliment is always an important but tricky part of culture. When it comes to American culture, you probably learned that it is polite to compliment someone's house especially when it's your first time visiting. It is also common to compliment someone's clothes or express (dramatically) how much you love the gift you just received. Sometimes, it may seem a little superficial and awkward for people whose own culture embraces "indirectness". Here is an alternative perspective for you to think about. If you want to compliment someone or something more often and directly, it actually requires us to observe a person or appreciate the details. Next time, even if your first impression of someone's home is just okay in your eyes, try to find something special in the house to compliment. The host/hostess will definitely take *it to heart and feel great that his/her effort is noticed. After all, who doesn't enjoy a compliment?*

文化角落

　　讚美一直是文化當中很重要但又有點棘手的部分。一提到美國文化，你可能已經學過，讚美他人的家是一個禮貌，尤其是初次拜訪時。讚美他人的衣服或表情（誇張地）表達你對於收到的禮物有多麼喜愛也是很普遍的事。有時候，對於一些文化上不直接表達感受的人來說，可能會覺得有點膚淺和奇怪。這裡提供另一個觀點給你參考。想要更加經常或是直接的讚美人事物時，其實需要我們懂得去觀察一個人或欣賞一些細節。下一次，即便他人的房子給你的第一印象是不怎麼樣的，試著從屋子裡找出有特色的點並給予讚美。屋子的主人絕對會欣然接受並因為他的巧思受到注意而感到開心。畢竟，誰不喜歡被讚美呢？

Scene 4

MP3 20

Suddenly, Tim receives a video call from his mother.

Tim — Hi Mom.

Tim's Mother — Hi sweetheart. How's summer camp going?

Tim — It's been very intense.

Tim's Mother — Who are those people behind you? They are all dressed up interestingly.

Tim — Errr... . they are actors and actresses. We are having a behind-the-scenes visit during the rehearsal of our play.

Tim's Mother — How fun! Oh, before I forget, Mr. Wizard sent you a package. The message on top of the package says, "Tim, keep up the good work! You may need these when you return." Should I open it for you?

Tim	No thanks, I'll open it later. Oh, I got to go now. Love you!
Tim's Mother	Love you! Bye.
Witch	(*pointing at Tim's phone*) I used to have one of those. I got it from Peter Pan as a Christmas gift. I loved it.
Tim	Oh yeah. This is what we call a smart phone. Sometimes it works just like magic!
Witch	I could not agree with you more!
Tim	By the way, do you know how I can get home? I wanna check out my package. Then I can also get Mr. Wizard's flour for the Giant. But the 'Essence of Rainbow' Magic Powder I have seems to only work within this world. I don't know how to go back to my world.
Witch	Hmmm... I think I know a portal for traveling to different worlds.

Tim & Giant ▸ Really? We're all ears.

Witch ▸ Well... I don't exactly remember the location, but perhaps that device in your hand can help me.

Tim ▸ My smart phone?

Witch ▸ (*smirking*) You know what? I do remember the location of the portal to transport you back to your world. But I'd like to make a deal with you.

Tim ▸ What's the deal?

Witch ▸ (*pointing at Tim's smart phone*) I'll tell you the portal's location in exchange for this magical tool.

Tim ▸ Deal.

The Witch leads them to a barn in the middle of the forest. In the barn, there is a ladder to the attic. After climbing up the ladder to the attic, they see a big long mirror covered by a piece of purple fabric with a golden 'R' embroidered in the middle.

第四場

忽然，提姆接到媽媽打來的視訊電話。

提姆 ▸ 嗨，老媽。

提姆的媽媽 ▸ 嗨，我的寶貝，夏令營如何呢？

提姆 ▸ 課程非常的密集。

提姆的媽媽 ▸ 你身後那群人是誰呢？他們的打扮都非常有趣。

提姆 ▸ 哦…他們是男演員和女演員，我們正在排練，順便做幕後參觀。

提姆的媽媽 ▸ 這麼有趣！喔，在我忘記之前跟你說，巫師先生寄給你一個包裹，包裹上的信息寫著「提姆，繼續保持下去！當你回來時可能需要這些東西。」我應該幫你打開來看嗎？

提姆 ▸ 不用，謝謝，我之後再打開，喔老媽，我該走了，愛你！

提姆的媽媽 ▸ 愛你！拜拜。

巫婆 ▸ （指著提姆的手機）我以前也有過一個像這樣的東西，是彼得潘送給我的聖誕節禮物，我很愛。

提姆 ▸ 是啊，這是所謂的智慧型手機，有時候用起來就像魔法一樣神奇！

巫婆 ▸ 我完全同意你的說法！

Act Four　Scene 4

提姆　對了，你知道如何送我回家嗎？我想要看我的包裹，也可以幫巨人跟巫師先生要麵粉，可是我有的這彩虹元素魔法粉末似乎只能在這世界使用，我不知道怎麼回去我的世界。

巫婆　恩…我想我知道一個通往不同世界的入口。

提姆&巨人　真的嗎？我們洗耳恭聽。

巫婆　那個嘛…我不記得確切的地點，不過或許你手上的設備可以幫我。

提姆　我的智慧型手機？

巫婆　（竊笑）你知道嗎？我正好想起來送你回你的世界的入口地點了，可是我要和你談個交易。

提姆　什麼交易？

巫婆　（指著提姆手上的智慧型手機）我跟你說入口的地點，來交換這魔法工具。

提姆　成交。

　　巫婆帶著他們到森林中的一個農舍，裡面有張通往閣樓的階梯，爬上階梯到閣樓之後，他們看到一面長長的大鏡子，上面蓋著一塊紫色的布，布的中間還刺了一個金黃色的英文字母 R。

Phrases & Sentence Patterns 慣用語 & 句型

❶ be dressed up 盛裝打扮

❷ used to + 原形動詞：過去曾經…

❸ This is what we call + 名詞：所謂…

❹ I cannot agree with you more！我完全同意你的說法！

❺ All ears. 洗耳恭聽

❻ make a deal with someone 與…交易

❼ in exchange for 交換

❽ "a big mirror covered by a piece of purple fabric" 或 "a golden 'R' embroidered in the middle" 的句型結構皆是「名詞＋過去分詞」，動詞由後面修飾前面的名詞，是一種被動式的表達方式

Cultural Note

During the Christmas season, you can find all kinds of Christmas holiday related products almost anywhere you shop. Christmas Vacation (1989) is one of the classic Christmas movies that you can find in many stores. The movie is about the Griswold family, who plans for a big family Christmas but it ends up being a big disaster. The movie starts out with Mr. Griswold, the father of the family, driving his family to a Christmas tree farm in the middle of nowhere to purchase the family Christmas tree. Of

Act Four Scene 4

course, the Christmas tree is at the center of all the accidents that happen to the family and their neighbors. One very funny moment involves Mr. Griswold being trapped in the attic when everyone else leaves the house to do Christmas shopping together. As a classic Christmas movie, the ending expresses the true spirit of Christmas, that is, what really matters is the family reunion and giving.

文化角落

　　聖誕季時，你可以在任何店家找到各式各樣有關聖誕假期的產品。你也可以在許多店家看到《聖誕假期》（Christmas Vacation）（1989）這部經典聖誕節電影。電影是有關格瑞斯烏德（Griswold）一家人，原本籌劃好的大家族相聚聖誕節，最後卻搞出一個大災難。電影一開始，一家之主的格瑞斯烏德先生開著車，載著家人去鳥不生蛋的聖誕樹農場買聖誕樹。當然，後來所有發生在家人和鄰居身上的意外，都圍繞在這棵聖誕樹。其中一個好笑的片段是，當所有人一起去採買聖誕節禮物時，格瑞斯烏德先生被困在閣樓裡。既然是一部經典聖誕節電影，故事結局即傳遞了真正的聖誕節精神，也就是，最重要的是，家人團圓和願意為他人付出。

Witch   *(pointing at the mirror)* There it is. Simply uncover and look into the mirror while thinking about your world. When the image of your world appears you must dive into it immediately. Be sure not to get sucked into another world.

Tim   Got it!

Witch   I must leave now in case I get sucked in by mistake. Good luck!

Tim   Thank you. *(He hands the Witch his smart phone.)* Here you go. I'll send you a text once I get home safely.

Looking into the mirror, both Tim and the Giant see many different worlds popping up one after another. The worlds are shifting faster than they can blink. Soon, they feel a forceful power pulling them into the mirror. Tim keeps watching attentively.

Tim   *(shouting to the Giant)* This is it... Go!

Both of them quickly jump into the mirror. At that moment, The Three Little Pigs, who had been napping in the attic, were startled by a boisterous noise. They slowly approach the mirror to investigate when suddenly, all Three Little Pigs disappear.

Man in Shadow — (*Watching Tim jump into the mirror using his Crystal Ball*) I can't allow him to ruin my big plans. (*He gives the Big Bad Wolf the order.*) Follow him now and bring me back the Three Little Pigs alive.

The Wolf — (*drooling*) Can I at least eat one if I get hungry on the way back?

Man in Shadow — Don't you dare bite off even one finger!

The Wolf — (*disappointed*) Yes Master.

Man in Shadow — By the way, let's turn the tables on these fella's and add some new twists to that little boy's fairytale world.

The Wolf — That should be as easy as pie! I will make him tremble in fear.

Man in Shadow ── Once the task is complete you can eat to your heart's content.

The Wolf ── (*mouth watering*) Anything?

Man in Shadow ── You name it!

The Wolf ── Woohoo!

 第五場

巫婆 ── （指著鏡子）就是這個，你只要揭開鏡子，看著鏡子時想著你的世界，當你的世界的影像出現時，要立刻跳進去，切記不要被捲進另一個世界裡。

提姆 ── 了解！

巫婆 ── 我現在必須要離開，以防不小心被吸進你的世界，祝你好運！

提姆 ── 謝謝你。（他遞給巫婆他的智慧型手機）拿去吧，我平安到家之後再傳簡訊給你。

　　看著鏡子，提姆和巨人看到許多不同世界一個個冒出來，世界移動的速度比他們眨眼來得快。不久，他們感受到一陣強大的力量將他們往鏡子裡面吸過去，提姆聚精會神地看著。

提姆 ─ （對巨人大喊）就這個了…走！

　　他們兩人快速地往鏡子裡跳。此時，正在閣樓睡午覺的三隻小豬被喧囂的聲音驚醒。他們慢慢的靠近鏡子，往鏡子裡瞧，瞬間，三隻小豬也跟著消失了。

影子人 ─ （從水晶球看著提姆跳進鏡子裡）我不能讓他壞了我的好事，（對壞心大野狼下命令）跟著他並且將三隻小豬活捉帶回來。

野狼 ─ （流口水）我可以至少吃一隻嗎？如果回程餓的話。

影子人 ─ 連一根手指頭都不准碰！

野狼 ─ （感到失望）是的，主人。

影子人 ─ 對了，我們來個扭轉局勢，加一些轉折到這小男孩的童話故事裡頭。

野狼 ─ 這應該易如反掌，我會讓他因為害怕而顫抖的。

影子人 ─ 你一旦達成任務之後，你可以吃任何想吃的東西吃到你心滿意足為止。

野狼 ─ （流口水）任何東西嗎？

影子人 ─ 只要你說得出來的都可以！

野狼 ─ 唷呼！

Phrases & Sentence Patterns慣用語 & 句型

❶ be sure（not）to + 原形動詞：一定（不）要

❷ in case 以防萬一

❸ Here you go.（遞東西給對方時）給你

❹ Don't you dare + 原形動詞：（用於警告）不准；你敢…就給我試看看

❺ turn the tables 扭轉局勢，反敗為勝

❻ easy as pie 輕而易舉的事，易如反掌

❼ to one's heart's content 直到心滿意足

❽ You name it. 只要你説的出來（都算數／都行／都有…）

Wolves are popular animals in fairy tales and fables. Based on the many stories about wolves, idioms were created to depict various situations. For example, when someone "cries wolf", it means the person is sending a false alarm of a danger, just like the shepherd boy in Aesop's Fables. Another expression is "keep the wolf from the door". Imagine that you have a friend who looks so tired. When you ask him, "What's up?" He replies, "Oh, I am working an extra shift every week to keep the wolf from the door." Can you guess what that means? Since people *have a stereotype that wolves are always hungry and looking for food, wolves represent poverty and starvation. Therefore, people want to avoid situations that are just as scary as a big hungry wolf. You may wonder if images of wolves are always bad. Well, Marvel's Wolverine is a superhero in American comic books who represents the power of the wolf in a different way.*

文化角落

　　野狼在童話故事和寓言故事裡都很受歡迎。俚語也根據許多有關野狼的故事因應而生以描述不同情況。舉例來說，當有人喊「狼來了」時，代表的是對方傳遞出有危險的假警告，就和伊索寓言裡那個放羊的孩子一樣。另一個用法是「讓野狼遠離門」。想像你有一個朋友看起很累，當你問他「怎麼了？」時，他回答「喔，我每週多排一次班，要讓野狼遠離門。」你猜得出來是什麼意思嗎？因為人們對野狼的刻板印象一直都是飢餓，四處尋找食物，所以野狼代表著貧窮與飢餓。因此，為了避免餓肚子，就像要躲避那令人害怕的飢餓大野狼。你可能會想，野狼的形象是不是都只有不好的？這麼嘛，*Marvel*（美國漫畫書公司）的金鋼狼在美國漫畫書裡是一個超級英雄，他以一個不同方式去詮釋了野狼的力量。

2
Part

Act Five 🎧 MP3 22

What's done is done...

Five years ago on Christmas Eve in the World of Wonderland, the Wizard decided to surprise the children with a magic show. He spent all day making a new magical potion. Finally, before the children were ready to open their gifts, he successfully created a potion that would bring the Nutcracker to life! That night, the Wizard's trick was a big hit and everyone had a blast at the party. The next morning, while the Wizard was in the middle of a dream, his butler rushed into the bedroom shouting...

Scene 1

Butler	Master! Something bad happened last night!
Wizard	(*Jumping out of his bed*) What is it?
Butler	The Nutcracker... he... errr... he badly wounded the Mouse King!
Wizard	What!? I 'd better get to the Mouse King's castle right away.

In the Kingdom of the Mouse, the Mouse King is lying in bed. His face is pale and his lips would occasionally quiver.

Mouse King	My dear Wizard! Look at what your magic has done to me!
Wizard	My friend, I am so sorry that my Nutcracker magic trick ended up putting you in this life-threatening situation.
Mouse King	I hope you didn't mean for this to happen.

Wizard — Of course not!

Mouse King — I was just joking. (*He coughs.*) Life has simply thrown me a curve.

Wizard — (*holding the Mouse Kings' paws*) Is there anything I can do for you?

Mouse King — During my reign, my mice have finally had an abundant supply of cheese allowing them to feed their families.

Wizard — Yes, indeed. The Dairy Queen has been very pleased to have established a stable business with your kingdom.

Mouse King — If something happens to me, please help my mice thrive and continue to have a good relationship with the humans.

Wizard — You'll be fine. I'll try my best to heal your wound.

Mouse King — (*smiling weakly*) We both know when Death summons us, there is no escape.

Wizard ▸ I'm so sorry.

Mouse King The only thing I wish I could change is the way the people outside the World of Wonderland perceives us. It bothers me a great deal that humans in that world still see us as dirty creatures.

Wizard ▸ Forget about it, my dear friend. You know you shouldn't have crossed to another world where humans are known to be unfriendly to you and your fellow mice.

Mouse King ▸ I know... but I love seeing the beautiful decorations during Christmas.

Wizard ▸ I agree. Those Christmas lights are very pretty. I enjoy going to that world also to see all the unusual things.

Mouse King ▸ (*coughing a little bit while laughing*) Yes, indeed.

Wizard ▸ Did you get a bite of gingerbread this time?

| Mouse King | Of course! I was savoring it slowly before your Nutcracker decided to pick a fight with me. |

| Wizard | Please forgive me my friend. |

第五幕

覆水難收…

　　五年前的聖誕節前夕，在魔幻世界，巫師決定藉由魔術秀給小孩子一個驚喜，他花了一整天在做新的魔法藥水，最後，當小孩子正準備要打開他們的禮物時，他成功地做出一個魔法藥水可以讓胡桃鉗活過來，那一個晚上，巫師的戲法成功地大受歡迎，而且每個人在派對上都玩得很盡興，隔天早上，當巫師還在睡夢中時，他的管家衝進房間並大喊…

第一場

| 管家 | 主人！昨晚發生大事了！ |

| 巫師 | （從床上跳起來）怎麼了？ |

| 管家 | 胡桃鉗…他…哦…他將鼠王傷得很嚴重。 |

| 巫師 | 什麼！？我得立刻趕去鼠王的城堡一趟。
在鼠國裡，鼠王正躺在床上，他的臉色蒼白，雙唇偶爾顫抖。 |

鼠王　我親愛的巫師！瞧你的魔法對我幹的好事啊！

巫師　我的朋友啊，真的對不起，我的胡桃鉗魔法把戲最後竟然置你於生命受到威脅的處境。

鼠王　但願你本來沒打算讓這一切發生。

巫師　當然沒有！

鼠王　開玩笑的啦！（咳了一下）我的人生只是丟了一個驚喜的變化球給我。

巫師　（握著鼠王的手）有任何我可以為你做的事嗎？

鼠王　在我的統治之下，我的鼠民終於擁有充足的起司，讓他們可以養家活口。

巫師　的確是這樣，冰雪皇后一直很高興可以和你的國家建立穩定的生意。

鼠王　萬一我發生不幸，請壯大我的鼠民並幫他們持續和人類保持良好的關係。

巫師　你會沒事的，我會盡我全力治癒你的傷口。

鼠王　（虛弱地微笑著）我倆都知道，當死神召喚時，逃也逃不掉的。

巫師　真的很對不起你。

鼠王 現在唯一一件我希望當初我有能力改變的是，魔幻世界之外的人類看待我們的方式，外頭的人類依舊視我們為骯髒的生物，這件事實在很令我困擾。

巫師 算了吧，我的朋友。你當初實在不應該跨越到另一個世界的，眾所皆知那裡的人類對你還有你的鼠民很不友善。

鼠王 我知道…可是我喜歡看聖誕節那些美麗的佈置。

巫師 我同意你說的，那些聖誕節的燈飾真的很漂亮，我也很喜歡去那世界看一些不尋常的東西。

鼠王 （邊笑邊咳）的確是這樣。

巫師 你這次有吃到一口薑餅嗎？

鼠王 當然有！在你的胡桃鉗決定找我挑釁鬧事前，我正在慢慢地品嚐薑餅。

巫師 請原諒我的朋友！

 Phrases & Sentence Patterns慣用語 & 句型

❶ bring to life 使甦醒
❷ a big hit 成功地大受歡迎
❸ have a blast 玩得很盡興
❹ end up 最後（處於…狀態）…；最後（成為）…；
❺ throw someone a curve 使驚訝（通常是突如其來的改變或麻煩事）

⑥ establish a stable business with… 建立穩定的生意

⑦ shouldn't have +p.p. 當初不應該…

⑧ pick a fight 挑釁鬧事

Cultural Note

　　The story "The Nutcracker and the Mouse King," written by Ernst Theodor Amadeus Hoffmann in 1816 is about a girl named Marie and her favorite Christmas toy, the nutcracker. On Christmas Eve, Marie's godfather Drosselmeyer, a clockmaker and an inventor, brings her and her siblings Christmas gifts, including a special Nutcracker. That night, she watches the Nutcracker come alive and fight with the evil Mouse King. The next day, her godfather tells Marie the story about how the Nutcracker was cursed and turned into a nutcracker. In the end, the curse is broken and the Nutcracker turns back into a young man when Marie promises to love the Nutcracker the way he is. Eventually, they get married and she becomes the queen of the doll kingdom. In 1982, the Russian composer Tchaikovsky adapted the story into a ballet. Today, The Nutcracker has gained popularity and is widely performed during the Christmas season in cities across the country. Try comparing

the adapted story told in the ballet to the original
as you enjoy the music and dance!

文化角落

　　恩斯特賀夫曼（*Ernst Theodor Amadeus Hoffman*）於 1816 年完成《胡桃鉗和老鼠王》，是關於瑪莉（*Marie*）和她最愛的聖誕節玩具（胡桃鉗）的故事。*Marie* 的教父卓斯爾梅爾（*Drosselmeyer*）是位鐘錶匠和發明家，他在平安夜那晚為她和她的兄弟姐妹帶了一些聖誕節禮物，包括胡桃鉗。當晚，她看到胡桃鉗醒過來，並和邪惡的老鼠王打鬥。隔天，她的教父告訴她，胡桃鉗為什麼會受到詛咒而變成一個胡桃鉗。後來，當瑪莉承諾會愛胡桃鉗的樣子時，詛咒被破解了，胡桃鉗再度變回成一位年輕的男子。最後他們倆人結婚，瑪莉成為玩具玩國的皇后。1982 年，俄國作曲家柴可夫斯基（*Tchaikovsky*）將故事改編成芭蕾舞劇，如今，胡桃鉗芭蕾舞劇在美國深受歡迎，許多城市都會在聖誕季節表演此劇。當你享受胡桃鉗芭蕾舞劇的音樂和舞蹈時，也可以試著比較改編後的故事和原著有何不同唷！

Act Five Scene 2

Scene 2   MP3 23

Mouse King — Forgive yourself. I am not afraid of death. We all will kick the bucket at some point. (*He suddenly finds himself short of breath.*) I... I... I believe I'm going to die soon.

Wizard — (*taking out a digital heart rate monitor and putting it around the Mouse King's wrist*) Let me use this magical device I got in Chicago to measure your heart. Whoa, your heart is beating crazy fast!

Mouse King — (*panting and trying to catch his breath*) I was just dreaming about eating some mouthwatering Gouda cheese.

Wizard — Hang in there and I'll get all the cheese you can eat after your recovery.

Mouse King — I feel my body is running out of fuel. Please take care of my family. Goodbye my friend. (*He closes his eyes.*)

Wizard — (*giving the Mouse King CPR*) Stay with me buddy!

Mouse Prince — (*rushing to his father's bedside and shouting at the Wizard*) What are you doing to my father?

Wizard — I'm giving him CPR.

Mouse Prince — You hypocrite! First your Nutcracker stabbed him and now you're beating him to death with your bloody hands!

Wizard — Oh no. These are just my red gloves. (*He removes his gloves.*) See, I have clean hands.

Mouse Prince — (*frantically shaking the Mouse King's body*) Papa! Don't leave us alone! Wake up!

Mouse King — (*opening his eyes suddenly*) Quiet, son! I want to die peacefully. Oh, now I die!

Then the Mouse King dies. The long beep sounding from the heart rate monitor is piercing throughout the room as everyone silently grieves.

Wizard → I am so sorry for your loss. Please accept my sincere condolences.

Mouse Prince → (*with grief and anger*) I don't need your crocodile tears! I will have my revenge for my father's death. Once I take over the World of Wonderland, I will cast a spell on the world where the humans are never friendly to us.

Wizard → Please... calm down.

Mouse Prince → (*shouting at the Wizard*) Get lost! NOW!

第二場

鼠王 → 原諒你自己吧，我不害怕死亡，我們總有一天都會掛掉的。（他忽然發現自己喘不過氣來）我…我…我相信我將要死去了。

巫師 → （拿出一個數位心跳監控器並將它套在鼠王的手腕上）讓我用我從芝加哥帶回來的神奇儀器幫你測量心跳。哇喔，你的心跳速度快得嚇人！

鼠王 → （上氣不接下氣地呼吸著）我剛夢到令人垂涎的高達（Gouda）起司。

巫師 ▸ 撐著點，等你康復之後，我會給你吃起司吃到飽。

鼠王 ▸ 我感覺到我的身體像是油燈枯盡，請照顧我的家人，永別了我的朋友。（他閉上眼睛）

巫師 ▸ （給鼠王做人工心肺復甦術）兄弟啊！保持清醒，別昏過去！

鼠王子 ▸ （衝到他父王的床邊並對巫師大叫）你對我父王做了什麼好事？

巫師 ▸ 我在對他做人工心肺復甦術。

鼠王子 ▸ 你這虛偽的傢伙！先是你的胡桃鉗刺傷他，現在你又用沾滿血的雙手打死他！

巫師 ▸ 喔不，這只是我的紅手套。（他脫掉他的手套）你看，我的雙手是乾淨無罪的。

鼠王子 ▸ （瘋狂地搖晃著鼠王的身體）爸爸！別離我們而去！醒醒啊！

鼠王 ▸ （忽然張開雙眼）安靜，鼠兒啊！我要平靜地死去，喔，我這就死去！
接著鼠王死了。從心跳監控器傳來的長長「嗶」聲刺穿了整個房間，每個人都無聲地哀悼著。

巫師 ▸ 你失去了你父親，對此讓本人深感遺憾，請你接受我誠摯的哀悼之意。

Act Five　Scene 2

鼠王子　（帶著悲傷與憤怒）我不需要你的貓哭耗子假慈悲！我會為我父王的死復仇的，等我佔領了魔幻世界之後，我會對那個對我們不友善的人類世界下咒語。

巫師　拜託…請冷靜下來。

鼠王子　（對著巫師大吼）現在立刻給我滾！

Phrases & Sentence Patterns慣用語 & 句型

❶ kick the bucket （非正式）死掉；翹辮子
❷ Hang in there.（鼓勵對方）堅持住；挺住
❸ stay with me（當對方要昏過去時）保持清醒，別昏過去！
❹ have clean hands 無罪的
❺ sincere condolence 誠摯的哀悼之意
❻ crocodile tears 貓哭耗子假慈悲
❼ take over 佔領；接管
❽ get lost（口語）滾

Cultural Note

There is another Mouse King in Anderson's fairy tale "Soup from a Sausage Peg." In Danish, the phrase "to cook soup from a sausage peg" means to make a big deal out of nothing. In the fairy tale, the Mouse King announces that the young female mouse who can make soup from the sausage peg will be his queen. Only four mice go out to look for the recipe. When they come back, they describe their adventures to the king one by one. The last mouse tells the Mouse King that the recipe is to boil a kettle of water and put in the sausage peg. Then, the Mouse King needs to stir the boiling water with his tail. It sounds dangerous, but the Mouse King agrees to do it. However, when his tail touches the hot steam, he jumps away from the kettle and announces immediately, "You must be my queen, and we will discuss this question again after our golden wedding (50 years later)!" Hence, the female mouse successfully tricks the Mouse King into marrying her! By the way, this classic story is also available on YouTube by typing the words "Sausage Peg Soup" in the search bar. If you have hard time understanding the story, remember to turn on the captions by clicking on the caption icon at the bottom right of the video!

文化角落

　　安徒生童話也有一個關於老鼠王的故事《香腸木釘煮成湯》（*Soup from a Sausage Peg*）。丹麥的俚語「香腸木釘煮成湯」是用來比喻大驚小怪的行為。在安徒生的童話故事裡，老鼠王對年輕母老鼠宣布，只要有辦法用香腸木釘熬成湯，即可成為他的皇后，結果只有四隻年輕母老鼠敢出去尋找食譜。等牠們回來之後，一一對老鼠王描述自己的冒險。最後一隻母老鼠對老鼠王說，食譜就是要燒開一壺滾燙的水，再放入香腸木釘，然後老鼠王必須用牠的尾巴攪拌滾水。聽起來很危險，但老鼠王還是同意這麼做。不過，等到牠的尾巴碰到熱騰騰的蒸氣時，牠立刻跳離那壺熱水並宣布「你就是我的皇后，煮湯這問題等我們金色婚禮（50 週年）再討論!」於是，這隻母老鼠成功地用計謀讓老鼠王娶她！對了，這經典的故事也可以在 *YouTube* 上找到影片，只要輸入 "*Sausage Peg Soup*" 搜尋即可，看影片時如果覺得英文聽不太懂，記得將影片右下角的字幕功能打開!

When two worlds meet...

The humans throughout the World of Wonderland send their condolences to the Mouse Prince for his loss. But once he's crowned the new Mouse King, he still chooses to end all communications and business with human beings. He befriends many other animals and trains them to be fierce fighters and killers, especially the wolves. The Wizard determines it would be best to leave the World of Wonderland after the Mouse King's death. He hopes that as long as he isn't in the World of Wonderland, the new Mouse King will forget about his plan for revenge. Unfortunately, that theory will prove to be very wrong.

 **Scene 1**

After a very bumpy ride through the clouds, Tim and the Giant fall out of the sky and land in Tim's backyard.

| Tim | Ouch, what a rough ride! |

| Giant | I think I'm having motion sickness. |

| Tim | Yay! I'm home! My home sweet home! C'mon on! Let's go to my room and unwrap my parcel! |

As the Giant picks himself up off the ground, the Three Little Pigs fall out of the sky one by one. Each pig lands on top of the Giant and knocks him down again.

| Tim | (*surprised and amused at the same time*) Are you three doing some kind of Chinese stunt now? |

| Giant | (*painfully reaching his hand out from the pile of pigs on top of him*) Oka-a-y. I call Uncle! He-e-e-lp! I-I-I'm fee-e-l-ing suffocated. |

The Three Little Pigs immediately climb down off the Giant.

Tim → (*To the Three Little Pigs.*) Where did you come from?

The Three Little Pigs → Oink-oink-aedi-oink-on-oink-evah-oink-ew-oink-oink.

Tim → All right. You're speaking Greek to me. (*He turns on his Siri and then talks to the Little Three Pigs.*) Can you talk to Siri? Perhaps she can translate your oink oink into English for me.

The Three Little Pigs → Oink-oink-ew-oink-era-oink-erehw-oink-oink.

Siri → Sorry, I cannot understand Piggese. Here is an online translation app to download.

After Tim downloads the app, he can finally understand Piggese.

The Three Little Pigs → We apologize for the trouble, but where are we?

Tim → Welcome to Chicago! This is my backyard. Are you the Three Little Pigs?

The Three Little Pigs — (*shouting Loudly*) Yes, sir. We're the Three Little Pigs, the best, of the best, of the best constructors. Oink.

Giant — Yeah yeah yeah. Stop being so dramatic! We hear you.

Tim — Shh... quiet down. You'll wake up my family and the neighbors!

The group quietly tiptoes up the stairs to Tim's room. Tim immediately opens the package from the Wizard.

第六幕

當兩個世界交會時…

　　整個魔幻世界的人類都對鼠王子的失去傳達了弔唁之意,只是他登基成為新鼠王之後,依舊選擇結束與人類的所有交流和生意往來,他和許多其他動物交朋友,並訓練他們成為兇猛的戰士和殺手,尤其是野狼們。在鼠王去世之後,巫師認為自己最好離開魔幻世界,他只希望,他不在魔幻世界可以讓新鼠王忘掉自己的復仇計畫。不幸地是,這推測著實錯得離譜。

在雲層裡一陣顛簸之旅之後，提姆和巨人從天空掉下來，跌落到提姆家的後院。

提姆 ▶ 哎唷，真是令人不舒服的一程！

巨人 ▶ 我想我暈車了。

提姆 ▶ 耶！我回到家了，我最甜蜜的家！來吧，一起到我房間去拆包裹！
當巨人要從地上爬起來時，三隻小豬一個接一個從天空掉下來，一一跌落在巨人身上，將巨人又撞倒在地。

提姆 ▶ （覺得驚訝又同時感到有趣）這是哪招，你們三隻現在是在表演某種中國雜耍特技嗎？

巨人 ▶ （痛苦地從身上的豬堆中伸出他的手）好…了，我投降，救…救命啊！我…我…我快窒息了！

三隻小豬立刻從巨人身上爬了下來。

提姆 ▶ （對著三隻小豬說）你們打哪兒來的？

三隻小豬 ▶ 哼哼－道知不－哼哼－也－哼哼－們我－哼哼。

提姆 ▶ 可以了，我完全聽不懂你們在說什麼。（他打開 Siri 並對三隻小豬說）可不可以對 Siri（iPhone 的人工智慧語音助理軟體）說呢？或許她知道如何將你們的哼哼哼翻譯成英文給我聽。

第一隻小豬　哼哼－裡哪－哼哼－在－哼哼－們我－哼哼。

Siri　很抱歉，我不懂豬語，這裡有個線上翻譯應用程式可以下載。
提姆下載了應用程式之後，終於聽得懂豬語了。

第一隻小豬　很抱歉造成你們的麻煩，不過我們在哪裡呢？

提姆　歡迎來到芝加哥！這是我家後院，你們是三隻小豬嗎？

三隻小豬　（齊聲大叫）是的，先生。我們是三隻小豬，是最優秀最優秀最優秀的營建商，哼。

巨人　是是是，不用這麼誇張，我們聽得很清楚。

提姆　噓…安靜，你們會吵醒我的家人和鄰居！
一群人安靜地踮著腳尖上樓到提姆的房間去，提姆立刻打開巫師寄來的包裹。

Phrases & Sentence Patterns 慣用語 & 句型

❶ motion sickness 暈車
❷ home sweet home 甜蜜的家（語意近似「金窩銀窩，還是不如自己的狗窩好」）
❸ pick oneself up （跌倒後或發生不幸後）站了起來
❹ one by one 一個接著一個
❺ knock him down 撞倒在地
❻ say Uncle 投降
❼ speaking Greek 聽不懂

❽ Stop being + 形容詞：停止某行為或情緒（通常 being 帶有暫時性的含義）

Cultural Note

The Three Little Pigs is perhaps one of the most well-known fairy tales in the world. There are multiple variations of the story. In one version, the first and second little pigs are caught and eaten by the wolf. The third little pig outsmarts the wolf, captures him in a cauldron of boiling water and eats him. In another version, the first and second little pigs run to the third little pig's home after the wolf blows their houses down. The wolf burns his butt after jumping down the chimney into the boiling water and runs away. Besides this story, there is a very catchy children's rhyme that people play with their kids while pinching the kid's toes one by one. That is, each little piggy represents a toe. After pinching the last toe you say "wee-wee-wee-wee all the way home," while tickling the child! Here are the words:

This little piggy went to market,
This little piggy stayed home,
This little piggy had roast beef,

This little piggy had none.
And this little piggy cried,
"Wee-wee-wee-wee-wee,"
All the way home.

文化角落

　　《三隻小豬》的故事或許是所有的童話故事裡頭，最廣為人知的其中一則。故事有許多不同版本。在一個版本裡，第一隻小豬和第二隻小豬都被大野狼吃掉了，第三隻小豬用智取，成功以一鍋滾燙的熱水抓到大野狼，並將大野狼吃掉。另一個版本中，第一隻小豬和第二隻小豬在大野狼吹垮他們的房子之後，紛紛跑到第三隻小豬的家，大野狼的屁股因為從煙囪跳進滾燙的熱水而燙傷，最後逃之夭夭。除了《三隻小豬》的故事之外，大人也喜歡和小孩玩一個琅琅上口的童謠遊戲，遊戲中大人會邊唱邊一一抓一下小孩的腳趾頭，每個腳趾頭都代表一隻小豬，在抓到最後那個腳趾頭後，你就說「哇一哇一哇一路哭回家」時，順便搔孩子的癢！全文如下：

　　這隻小豬去市場，
　　這隻小豬待在家，
　　這隻小豬烤牛肉，
　　這隻小豬什麼都沒有，
　　然後這隻小豬正在哭，
　　哇-哇-哇-哇-哇
　　一路哭回家。

Tim opens the package and finds a glowing Crystal Ball! He removes the Crystal Ball from the parcel and places it on the floor. A projected image of the Wizard suddenly appears in the air and speaks to Tim.

Wizard   Hi Tim! I am pleased that you found your way back to Chicago! By this time, I'm sure that you know my true identity and you probably have millions of questions you want to get off your chest.

Tim   (*in protest*) Yeah, you could've told me more details before I left.

Wizard   Hahaha! Sorry about that. I just thought you might enjoy the surprise!

Tim   Can I visit you tomorrow morning?

Wizard   I'm afraid not. The World of Wonderland is in crisis, and I am out of town taking care of it.

Tim   When will you be back?

Wizard ▸ Hmmm... I'm not sure yet.

Tim ▸ Bummer!

Wizard ▸ If we can meet up, I will answer all your questions. If I can't make it back in time, I will need you to return to the World of Wonderland soon.

Giant ▸ (*shocked*) What!!!! You must make it back! Otherwise, how am I supposed to get the magical flour! (*He starts to whine.*) I'm doomed to be a dwarf forever!

Tim ▸ Knock it off! Don't you see? If the World of Wonderland is gone, how small you are won't matter any more. You won't even have a home to go back to!

Giant ▸ (*burying his face in a pillow*) Oh no! I'll be trapped in this tiny body AND stuck in this world forever.

Tim ▸ (*turning on his laptop on the desk* and *showing a YouTube channel to the Giant*) Calm down!

Why don't you sit down here and watch some cooking shows?

Giant — Cooking shows? Okay, I think I can do that. Sorry to make a spectacle of myself. I will try to be as cool as a cucumber now.

Tim — Attaboy!

提姆打開包裹後看到裡頭有一個發光的水晶球！他將水晶球從包裹裡拿出來放在地上，巫師的影像突然投射在空中並對著他說話。

巫師 — 嗨，提姆！我很高興你有找到辦法回到芝加哥來！到現在我肯定你已知道我的真實身份，你可能也有很多問題不吐不快。

提姆 — （抗議中）是啊，你大可在我離開前先多跟我說一些細節。

巫師 — 哈哈哈！真是抱歉，我只是覺得你會享受驚喜的過程！

提姆 — 我明天可以去找你嗎？

巫師 ▶ 恐怕沒辦法，魔幻世界正陷入危機，我出城去處理一些事情。

提姆 ▶ 你什麼時候回來？

巫師 ▶ 恩…我還不確定。

提姆 ▶ 真糟糕哩！

巫師 ▶ 如果我們可以碰面，我會回答你所有的問題。如果我沒辦法及時回去，我需要你盡快回到魔幻世界。

巨人 ▶ （感到震驚）什麼！！！你必須要回來啊！不然，我是該怎麼拿到魔法麵粉呢！（他開始哀哀叫）喔不，我註定一輩子都要當小矮人了！

提姆 ▶ 別鬧了！你難道不懂嗎？如果魔幻世界消失了，你個頭多小都無所謂了，你甚至會無家可回！

巨人 ▶ （將他的臉埋在枕頭裡）喔不！我將被困在這小小的身體裡，而且還被永遠困在這一個世界。

提姆 ▶ （開啟他書桌上的筆電並開了一個 YouTube 頻道給巨人看）冷靜下來！你何不坐在這裡，看一下美食節目呢？

巨人 ▶ 美食節目！？好吧，我想我辦得到，真抱歉剛才失態了，我現在會盡力像小黃瓜一樣冷靜的。

提姆 ▶ 乖！好棒唷！

Phrases & Sentence Patterns慣用語 & 句型

❶ get off one's chest 不吐不快

❷ in crisis 陷入危機

❸ in time 即時

❹ be doomed to（通常是不好的事）註定…

❺ knock it off 別吵了；別鬧了

❻ make a spectacle of oneself 失態

❼ as cool as a cucumber 像小黃瓜一樣的冷靜；（出奇地）冷靜

❽ attaboy 幹得好！很棒很乖！用來表達讚美，鼓勵，支持一個男孩子，男人，或公的動物，與 "That's the boy！" 同意）

Cultural Note

The Cloud Gate Sculpture, aka The Chicago "Bean", is located in Millennium Park. It is one of the most popular landmarks in Chicago. Made of highly polished stainless steel plates, the "Bean" reflects the beautiful skyline of Chicago. Thus, if you take a picture in front of it, you will be able to capture Chicago's beautiful skyline in the background! However, it does get extremely busy during weekends, so it's better to visit the "Bean" during a weekday so you don't have many tourists in the reflection. Millennium Park is also a good place to start exploring downtown Chicago. You can *visit the nearby Art Institute of Chicago, enjoy the Chicago architecture river cruise, go shopping on Michigan Avenue, or take a walk to enjoy the views along the banks of Lake Michigan. Depending on your plans, you can also purchase 1-Day, 3-Day, 7-Day, or 30-Day unlimited ride transit passes. With the pass, you can hop on any buses or take the "L"(short for "elevated" train) anywhere you want to go!*

文化角落

位於芝加哥千禧公園的雲門雕像（*The Cloud Gate Sculpture*），也稱為「芝加哥豆子」，是芝加哥最著名的地標之一。由磨到很光滑的不鏽鋼鐵板所建造的「豆子」映照著芝加哥美麗的天際線。因此，站在「豆子」面前拍照的話，芝加哥美麗的天際線就會成為照片的背景！不過，由於這「豆子」在週末時非常受歡迎，最好挑選平日時間去參觀，不然其他旅客也會變成照片裡的背景。千禧公園也是逛芝加哥市區的很好起點，你可以參觀附近的「芝加哥藝術學院」，搭渡輪享受芝加哥建築之旅，在密西根大道逛街，或是沿著密西根湖的沿岸散步。也可以根據自己的行程買無限次數的交通搭乘卡，有 1 天、3 天、7 天、和 30 天的方案可選擇，有了一張卡在手，就可以任意跳上任何公車，或是搭乘 "*The L*"（高架地鐵的簡稱），通行無阻。

Wizard — Check out the items in the parcel. You will need them at some critical moments.

Tim — (*picking up a cape and freaking out*) Whaa... aat's going on? Where are my hands!?

Wizard — (*laughing widely*) You're holding an invisibility cape. Let go of it and you will find your hands back.

Tim — (*kissing both hands*) Muuuuuahhhh! I love you guys!

Wizard — Did you see a piece of paper with an address and a digital key in the parcel?

Tim — Got them!

Wizard — Excellent! It's the address to my place in the World of Wonderland. Use your GPS and other technological gadgets in your backpack to guide you to my place.

Tim ▸ How about this digital key?

Wizard ▸ It is a key to my secret chamber. To enter, just swipe the key on the sensor pad. You will be in awe of what I have stored in that room.

Tim ▸ Looks like someone has something up his sleeve!

Wizard ▸ Haha, I am a wizard after all!

Tim ▸ Is there anything particular that you want me to find in that secret chamber?

Wizard ▸ Nope. Just use your creativity and make everything useful.

Tim ▸ C'mon! Stop beating around the bush! Please just tell me.

Wizard ▸ Quit your whining. This is a pre-recorded video. I can't answer your question since I didn't think of it in advance.

Tim ▸ Fine! You owe me big time!

Wizard ▸ By the way, be aware of potential enemies that might try to ambush you from now on! Good luck!

Then the Wizard's image disappears.

Tim ▸ (*turning to everyone in his room*) All right guys. Bed time! I have many things to pack tomorrow morning! (*He looks at two of the Little Pigs.*) Where's your brother?

Third Little Pig ▸ (*appearing suddenly in front of Tim*) Peek-a-boo! Oink.

Everyone is immediately startled and then they all laugh.

Tim ▸ Man, this invisibility cape is great! (*He puts the cape in his backpack.*) Ok, lights out!

第三場

巫師　看一下包裹裡的東西，在某些關鍵時刻你會需要用到的。

提姆　（拿出一件斗篷並且嚇到）發…生…什麼事了？我的雙手在哪裡？

巫師　（狂笑）你拿著一件隱形斗篷，放開它你的手就會回來了。

提姆　（親著雙手）啾啾啾咪！我愛你們！

巫師　你有看到包裹裡一張寫著地址的紙和一把數位鑰匙嗎？

提姆　找到了！

巫師　太棒了！這是我在魔幻世界的住家地址，用你的衛星導航（GPS）和背包裡的科技小玩意去找到我家吧。

提姆　這數位鑰匙是要做什麼的？

巫師　那是通往我家密室的鑰匙，你要打開密室的話，只需要將鑰匙在感應墊上刷一下。你會很讚嘆我收藏在那房間的物品。

提姆　看來某人暗中還準備了其他計畫！

巫師　哈哈，畢竟我是巫師啊！

提姆	有要我從密室找什麼特別的東西嗎？

巫師	沒有，你只需要發揮你的創造力，讓所有東西變得有用途。

提姆	拜託！別再拐彎抹角了！請直接跟我說。

巫師	別哀哀叫了，這是一個預錄的錄影帶，既然我沒有事先想到，我沒有辦法回答你。

提姆	算了！你欠我一份大人情！

巫師	對了，從現在開始要留意任何可能會突襲你的潛在敵人！祝你好運！

然後巫師的影像消失了。

提姆	（轉向房間所有的人）好啦，各位。睡覺時間到了！我明早還有一堆東西要打包！（他看著兩隻小豬）你們的兄弟呢？

第三隻小豬	（突然出現在提姆面前）哇！我在這裡！哼。每個人都立刻被嚇到然後又隨即笑了出來。

提姆	天啊，這隱形斗篷太讚了！（他將隱形斗篷放進他的背包）好了，熄燈！

Phrases & Sentence Patterns慣用語 & 句型

❶ let go of something 放開…鬆手
❷ be in awe of 驚嘆

❸ have something up one's sleeve 暗中還準備其他計畫；暗中有不同意見

❹ after all 畢竟

❺ in advance 事前；事先

❻ you owe me big time 你欠我一份大人情

❼ be aware of 留意；注意

❽ from now on 從現在起

Cultural Note

Children's songs and nursery rhymes can be heavily culturally specific. If you were not born in that country, you might have never heard of them. One of the common children's nursery rhymes in the United States is "Itsy-Bitsy Spider." The lyrics are silly but easy to sing along.

The itsy-bitsy spider
Climbed up the water spout
Down came the rain
And washed the spider out
Out came the sun
And dried up all the rain
And the itsy-bitsy spider
Climbed up the spout again

This song is usually performed while using hand gestures, which you can easily find on YouTube to learn if desired. On the other hand, some children's songs are universally popular, and all you need to learn is the lyrics! For example, "Two Tigers" in Chinese becomes "Brother John" in the English version. Try singing "Brother John" right now!

Are you sleeping,
Are you sleeping?
Brother John,
Brother John?
Morning bells are ringing,
Morning bells are ringing.
Ding Ding Dong,
Ding Ding Dong.

文化角落

兒歌和童謠可能帶有濃厚的文化特殊性。如果你不是在那國家出生長大，可能完全沒有聽過。美國文化裡一首耳熟能詳的童謠叫做「伊茲-比茲-蜘蛛」，很好笑但也很容易琅琅上口跟著唱。

伊茲比茲蜘蛛
爬上了排水管

天空降下了雨
將蜘蛛沖下來
太陽升起來
曬乾所有的雨
然後伊茲比茲蜘蛛
再度爬上排水管

　這首歌通常會搭配手勢，如果想要的話，上 *YouTube* 影片就可以學。另外，一些童謠是眾所皆知很受歡迎的，你只要學習當地歌詞就行!例如，中文的《兩隻老虎》英文版叫做《強尼兄弟》，你現在就可以試著唱看看!

你在睡覺嗎，
你在睡覺嗎?
強尼兄弟，
強尼兄弟?
早安鈴聲已響，
早安鈴聲已響。
叮叮咚，
叮叮咚。

The next morning Tim introduces his friends to his family.

Tim's Mother — You should've told me you would bring friends home. We are running out of groceries.

Tim — We can all go shopping together. I need to buy several things too.

Tim's Mother — Sounds good. Oh, are these pigs from Iowa? I have been dying to have an Iowa pork chop for a while!

The Three Little Pigs panic and shake their heads. Tim shows his mother the translation in the app on his phone so they can talk to the Three Little Pigs to reduce their anxiety.

Tim's Mother — (*smiling*) It's very nice to meet you, Three Little Pigs from the World of Wonderland. Don't worry, I was just cracking a joke. I would never eat Tim's friends.

Tim — Yeah, don't be so insecure. The fiercest animals

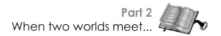
in this neighborhood are the raccoons and I don't think they eat pig. I guarantee you will find no trace of wolves around here.

Tim's Mother ► Hmm... why don't you watch the house for us while we're gone?

The Three Little Pigs smile and nod in agreement.

Giant ► Mrs. BeauDaring, can I go with you? This is my first visit to Chicago.

Tim's Mother ► Oh, you must be one of the Seven Dwarfs. How cute! Of course you can come along.

Giant ► Actually, I am not a dwarf but thank you for allowing me to go with you.

Tim shows the Three Little Pigs how to make an emergency phone call. Tim's Mother, Tim and the Giant enter the garage and pile into the car. Tim picks up the Giant and straps him into a child safety seat.

Giant ► (*kicking his feet in protest*) I don't want to sit in a baby's seat!! I am a giant!

Tim's Mother   I wish I could let you sit in the adult seat, but it's for safety's sake.

Tim   (*chucking*) Sorry dude. When in Rome, do as the Romans. Your size makes you look like a toddler here!

Tim's Mother   Ok. Make sure you both buckle up. Let's go shopping!

第四場

隔天早上提姆介紹他的朋友給家人認識。

提姆的媽媽 你應該早點跟我說你會帶朋友回來的。我們家都沒菜了。

提姆 可以大家一起去購物。我也需要買一些東西。

提姆的媽媽 好提議，喔，這些豬是從愛荷華來的嗎？我超想吃愛荷華的烤豬排，已經想了好一陣子了！
三隻小豬驚恐地搖著頭。提姆給他媽媽看手機上的翻譯應用程式，這樣他們才可以和三隻小豬溝通，以降低小豬們的焦慮。

提姆的媽媽 （笑笑著說）非常高興認識你們，來自魔幻世界的三隻小豬。別擔心，我只是對你們開了一個玩笑，我從來不吃提姆的朋友。

提姆 ▶ 是啊，別這麼沒安全感，在這附近最兇猛的動物是浣熊吧，我想他們不吃豬的，我保證你不會在這附近找到野狼的蹤跡。

提姆的媽媽 ▶ 恩…你們可以在我們出門的時候，幫我們看家嗎？
三隻小豬微笑並點頭同意。

巨人 ▶ 博德林太太，我可以和你們一起去購物嗎？這是我第一次造訪芝加哥。

提姆的媽媽 ▶ 喔，你應該是七個小矮人的其中一位吧，真可愛！你當然可以和我們同行。

巨人 ▶ 其實，我不是小矮人，不過謝謝你讓我一起去。
提姆教三隻小豬如何打緊急電話。博德林太太、提姆和巨人走去車庫準備上車，提姆抱起巨人，並將他安置在兒童安全座椅上，扣好安全帶。

巨人 ▶ （踢著雙腳抗議著）我不要坐在嬰兒安全座椅上！我是巨人！

提姆的媽媽 ▶ 但願我可以讓你坐在成人的位置，可是這是為了你的安全著想！

提姆 ▶ （呵呵笑）老兄不好意思，你要入境隨俗啊，你的身材在這世界看起來就像是一個幼兒啊！

提姆的媽媽 ▶ 好，確認一下你們都扣上安全帶了，咱們去購物了！

Phrases & Sentence Patterns慣用語 & 句型

❶ be dying to do sth 極想做…

❷ crack a joke 開玩笑

❸ come along 隨行一起去哪裡

❹ make an emergency phone call 撥打緊急電話

❺ I wish I could, but…但願我可以…，可是

❻ for the sake of 為了安全起見

❼ When in Rome, do as the Romans. 入境隨俗

❽ buckle up 扣上安全帶

Cultural Note

When you visit any state in the United States (US), people may suggest that you must try certain foods. For example, Boston, Massachusetts (along the coast in the Northeast United States), is famous for its New England clam chowder and Maine lobster. If you go to Chicago, Illinois (a state in the Midwest [Central] United States), you don't want to miss trying Chicago-style deep dish pizza or a Chicago Dog. In Iowa, the state just west of Illinois, citizens are particularly proud of their pork products (try their giant breaded pork tenderloins) and sweet corn on the cob. This is why the Three

Little Pigs reminded Tim's mother of the delicious Iowa Pork Chop in the story. If you travel to Texas (in the South region of the US), your belly will feel satisfied and stuffed when you try the smoked beef brisket or other Texas-style barbeque. Authentic Mexican food is also available in many cities in Texas, like in San Antonio. Finally, along the Western Coast of the United States, you can find various restaurants with specialties involving seafood. Their prosperous wine region (Napa Valley) also gives wine lovers a chance to visit some great vineyards. Once you have experienced all the famous dishes listed in your travel book, try to make friends with local people. They may surprise you with their homemade foods or have advice for some wonderful, not well-known, local cuisine!

　　在美國拜訪任何一州時，可能會有人建議你一定要試看看某些食物。譬如，在麻州（Massachusetts）的波士頓（沿著美國的東北海岸線）就得嚐嚐有名的新英格蘭蛤蠣濃湯和緬因龍蝦。如果你到位於美國中西部伊利諾利州（Illinois）的芝加哥，絕對不能錯過芝加哥風格的深碟披薩（deep dish pizza）或是芝加哥熱狗。在伊利諾利州（Illinois）隔壁的愛荷華州，當地人對於自己的豬肉產品特別感到自豪，可以試看看很大份量的滾麵包粉料理的里肌肉和一根根的甜玉米。這也就是為什麼三隻小豬讓提姆的媽媽想起愛荷華美味的豬排。如果你一路南下到德州，當你吃了煙燻牛肉片或是德州式烤肉後，你的肚子會感到又滿足又很脹。德州很多城市，像是聖安東尼奧（San Antonio），也可以吃到道地的墨西哥料理。最後，沿著美國西岸，可以找到很多提供特別海鮮料理的餐廳。蓬勃發展的釀葡萄酒區（納帕谷）也提供葡萄酒愛好者一些造訪葡萄園的機會。一旦你嚐盡旅遊書裡所有有名的菜餚之後，也可以試著和當地人交朋友。你可能會因為他們所做的家庭料理，或是告訴你一些很好吃，但不是那麼多人知道的當地料理而感到驚喜！

Scene 5 🎧 MP3 28

The Three Little Pigs are sniffing around the house in search of some food when they hear the doorbell.

First Little Pig — (*walking up to the front door*) I think there's somebody at the door.

The Wolf — (*faking as a salesman*) Knock knock.

First Little Pig — Who's there?

The Wolf — A salesman.

Second Little Pig — A salesman who?

The Wolf — A salesman who sells the best snacks in the world!

When the First Little Pig is about to open the door, the Third Little Pig stops him.

Third Little Pig — Thanks, but we don't care for any snacks. (*He whispers to his brothers.*) Cautious brothers. He

could be a wolf in salesman's clothes.

The Wolf — (*mumbling to himself*) I should just break in and eat them all!

Ten minutes later, the doorbell rings again.

Second Little Pig (*nervously*) I think he's back.

The Second Little Pig suddenly feels that his knees are weak and decides to sit down. He accidentally sits on the TV remote and turns it on. A movie scene with two groups of cowboys in a gunfight is playing and the volume is set on high!

The Wolf — (*ducking behind the tree*) No way! They've already learned how to use those deadly weapons? Ugh... I need an alternative plan!

An hour later, the Three Little Pigs smell the scent of grilled corn in the backyard.

First Little Pig — What is that? It smells so good!

Second Little Pig — I am starving.

Third Little Pig That smell is too tempting! Let's try to grab some and get back inside the house as fast as we can.

Upon seeing the grilled corn, the Three Little Pigs quickly become distracted and completely leave their plan behind.

First Little Pig (*speaking with a mouthful of corn*) This corn is heavenly!

Second Little Pig (*with a content smile on his face*) This is just as sweet as the cooking show we watched last night with the Giant described. Iowa sweet corn is well deserving of its reputation!!

Third Little Pig Let's ask Tim to pick up some more from the store. (*He makes a phone call.*) Oink oink. Tim! The corn is so delicious. Can you get more for us?

Tim What corn? Where did it come from?

Third Little Pig On the grill in your backyard! (*He looks up.*) Uh-oh... the Wolf is... He-elp!

The phone drops to the ground.

Tim ► Hello! Hello! Pig... are you there?

門鈴響時，三隻小豬正在家裡聞來聞去尋找吃的東西。

第一隻小豬 ► （走到前門）我想門外有人。

野狼 ► （假扮成一個推銷員）叩叩叩。

第一隻小豬 ► 是誰？

野狼 ► 推銷員。

第二隻小豬 ► 什麼推銷員？

野狼 ► 販賣全世界最好吃的零食的推銷員！
當第一隻小豬正準備開門時，第三隻小豬阻止他。

第三隻小豬 ► 謝謝，不過我們不愛吃零食。（他小聲地對哥哥們說）
哥，謹慎小心一些，他可能是野狼喬扮成推銷員。

野狼 ► （自言自語）我應該直接闖入，將他們全部吃掉！

10 分鐘之後，門鈴又響了。

第二隻小豬 ► （很緊張）我想他又回來了。

　　第二隻小豬忽然一陣腳軟，於是決定坐下來，他意外地坐在一個遙控器上面，並轉開了電視。電影正在播放雙方牛仔們的槍戰，音量還調到很大聲！

野狼　什麼！他們已經學會該怎麼使用致命武器了？啊…我需要備案！
一小時之後，三隻小豬聞到後院傳來的一陣陣烤玉米香味。

第一隻小豬　那是什麼？聞起來真香！

第二隻小豬　我快餓扁了。

第三隻小豬　這香味太吸引人了！我們去拿一些，然後盡快地回到屋內。
當三隻小豬看到烤玉米時，很快地就分心了，完全將他們的計劃拋諸腦後。

第一隻小豬　（滿嘴塞滿玉米地説話）這玉米真是人間美味啊！

第二隻小豬　（臉上帶著滿足的微笑）這玉米就像我們昨天和巨人一起看的美食節目上説的一樣甜，愛荷華玉米真的實至名歸！

第三隻小豬　我們請提姆再從店裡買一些回來吧。（他打電話）哼哼，提姆！玉米真好吃，你可以再帶一些回來給我們嗎？

提姆　什麼玉米？哪來的？

第三隻小豬　你家後院的烤肉架上的！（他抬頭往上看）阿喔…野狼他…救命啊！

電話掉到地上。

提姆 哈囉！哈囉！豬仔…你還在聽嗎？

Phrases & Sentence Patterns慣用語 & 句型

❶ in search for 尋找

❷ care for 喜歡

❸ a wolf in salesman's clothes（改編自 "A wolf in sheep's clothes." 披著羊皮的狼）

❹ break in 非法闖入屋內；闖空門

❺ knees are weak 兩腳發軟

❻ No way！不可能！決不！

❼ Leave something behind 遺忘…；將…拋諸腦後

❽ well deserve of one's reputation. 實至名歸

Cultural Note

A word game is one of the most challenging games for foreign language learners. Learners not only need to accumulate enough vocabulary but also need to get the underlying meanings when the puzzles are cultural specific. A good example is the crossword puzzles that appear in the daily newspaper. The player must figure out the right answers by reading each hint. If crosswords puzzles seem to be intimidating, perhaps you would like to try "Knock Knock Jokes" to practice some English words first. It takes two people to play a "Knock Knock Joke" and they always start with one person saying, "Knock Knock". Then the counterpart replies, "Who's there?" In the end, the first person will end the game by describing the characteristics or the situations or making a funny comment related to the person, the object, or the idea. Below are a couple of examples.

Example 1
Knock, Knock!
Who's there?
Boo.
Boo who?
Don't cry, it's just a joke.

Example 2
Knock, Knock!
Who's there?
Cows go.
Cows go who?

No, cows go moo!

文化角落

　　文字遊戲對於外語學習者而言是極富挑戰性的遊戲之一。學習者不但需要累積一定量的單字，也需要了解帶有文化特殊性的謎語所要傳遞的解言下之意。每日報紙上的猜字謎遊戲就是一個很好的例子。玩遊戲的人必須從提示當中想出正確的答案。如果猜字謎遊戲令你望而生畏，或許可以試著先以「敲敲門笑話」練習玩英文文字遊戲。玩這遊戲需要兩個人才行，一開始時其中一個人會說「敲敲門」，另一方回答「誰在門外？」最後，起頭的那一個人要針對所提出的人事物或點字，描述其特性，或是情況，或是下一個好笑的結論來結束這遊戲。以下是兩個例子：

例子 1

敲敲門！誰在門外？

噓 誰在噓？

別哭，我只是在開你玩笑。（註：*boo* 對某人表示不滿時所發出的聲音）

例子 2

敲敲門！誰在門外？

牛在叫。牛在叫誰？

不是啦，牛叫哞哞！

 ★ ★ 🎧 MP3 29

The phone is still on and Tim overhears the Wolf's conversation with the Three Little Pigs.

The Wolf Throughout centuries, my ancestors have taught us to beware of you tricky little pigs. Today, I've finally broken the curse! (*He howls and does a little wolf dance.*) Hoowooooo!

Third Little Pigs Alright, you've proven that you can outsmart us! How about you release us now?

The Three Little Pigs are squirming in the net.

The Wolf (*smirking slyly*) Not a chance my old enemies. But don't worry. I won't even lick one of your tasty little fingers... ye-e-et! Not until you complete the mission my master has in store for you.

First Little Pig What mission? We're just ordinary pigs!

The Wolf Oh, don't be so humble. You pigs are great

builders of houses and castles.

Third Little Pigs (*shaking his head*) No. We're actually VERY BAD builders!

Second Little Pig Remember how your ancestor blew down our ancestor's houses?

The Wolf Yeah, but I'm sure your ancestor's passed on to you the skills to build strong brick houses. Anyway, let's not waste our breath debating. It's time to get back to the World of Wonderland! Hoowoooooo!

First Little Pig Wait a minute! Can you at least give me another ear of corn before we go?

The Wolf As you wish. (*He talks to himself.*) The chubbier you get, the happier I will be!

Tim then hears only silence from the phone. He asks his mother to take him home immediately and describes what he heard over the phone on the way. When they arrive home, Tim sprints to the backyard only to find the phone and some half-eaten corn on the ground.

Giant ▶ (*eating the rest of the corn*) Wow! This corn is delicious. No wonder the pigs got hooked on it. Mrs. BeauDaring, can we have some sweet corn for dinner tonight?

Tim's mother nods but can barely smile.

Tim ▶ Oh, mom! I just got a text from Mr. Wizard. He's back. I'll be home in time for dinner!

Mom ▶ Why don't you take your little friend with you?

The Giant ▶ (*grumbling to himself*) Pfft... little?

Tim ▶ Okie dokie!

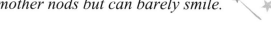

第六場

電話還未掛斷，提姆偷聽到野狼和三隻小豬的對話。

野狼 ▶ 幾個世紀以來，我的祖先一直教導我們要小心你們這些狡猾的小豬，今天，我終於打破詛咒了！（他狼嚎一聲並跳起狼之舞）嚎～嗚！

第三隻小豬 ▶ 好啦，你已經證明你比我們聰明，放我們走如何呢？
三隻小豬在網子裡蠕動著。

野狼　（狡猾地賊賊笑著）想都別想，我的宿敵，不過別擔心，我連舔都不會舔一下你那可口的小指頭…暫時！直到你們完成我的主人為你們準備好的任務。

第一隻小豬　什麼任務？我們只是平凡的豬！

野狼　喔，不要如此謙虛。豬是蓋房子和城堡的厲害建築工人。

第三隻小豬　（搖頭）不是啊，我們其實是非常糟的建築工人。

第二隻小豬　記得你的祖先是怎樣吹倒我們祖先的房子嗎？

野狼　是啦，不過我很確定的是，你們的祖先也同時傳授了如何蓋堅固磚屋的技術，總之，我們不要再浪費唇舌辯論了，差不多該回魔幻世界了，嚎～嗚！

第一隻小豬　等一下！在我們離開之前，你可以至少再給我一根玉米嗎？

野狼　如你所願。（對自己說）你吃得越胖，我越開心！
提姆接著只聽到電話那頭一陣沈默，他請他媽媽立刻載他回家，並在回程路上描述了一下他在電話這頭所聽到的一切，當他們到家時，提姆衝到後院，只在地上找到電話和一些吃了一半的玉米。

巨人　（吃起剩下的玉米）哇！這玉米真好吃，難怪豬仔們整個愛上了，博德林太太，我們今晚的晚餐可以有些甜玉米嗎？
提姆的媽媽點頭，但幾乎擠不出笑容。

| 提姆 | 喔，老媽！我剛收到巫師先生傳來的簡訊，他回來了，我會在吃晚餐之前回來！ |

| 提姆的媽媽 | 你何不帶著你的小朋友一起去呢？ |

| 巨人 | （嘟囔著）嘖…小？ |

| 提姆 | 好的！ |

Phrases & Sentence Patterns慣用語 & 句型

❶ not a chance 一點機會都沒有；想都別想
❷ in store for 等待著；即將發生
❸ pass on 傳授下去
❹ waste one's breath：浪費唇舌
❺ an ear of corn 一根玉米
❻ on the way 在路上
❼ get hooked on something 迷上某事
❽ okie dokie（口語）好

Cultural Note

The Princess Bride(1987), a classic American romantic comedy movie, is a fairy tale adventure about Princess Buttercup and her true love Westley. The beautiful Buttercup considers herself much better than the farm boy, Westley, who she treats in a scornful manner at every turn. Whenever Buttercup gives him an order, Westley always replies, "As you wish." Later, she realizes that Westley's "as you wish" actually means "I love you" and she's in love with him, too. In order for them to marry, Westley decides he must leave town to seek fortune at sea. He promises her that he will come back to marry her someday. However, Westley's ship is attacked by the Dread Pirate Roberts and Westley is presumed dead. About five years later, Princess Buttercup agrees to marry Prince Humperdinck, even though she doesn't love him. However, she is kidnapped by bad guys before the wedding. After a dangerous journey, the princess is rescued by the man in black, who she presumes is the Dread Pirate Roberts. Confessing she doesn't love Prince Humperdinck and revealing to the Dread Pirate Roberts that he killed her one true love, she tells him that she wishes he'd die too and shoves him down a hill. While tumbling down the hill and yelling, "As you wish," soon she discovers he is actually Westley!

文化角落

　　美國經典浪漫愛情喜劇《公主新娘》（The Princess Bride）（1987）是一部關於牛奶杯公主（Princess Buttercup）和他的真愛衛斯理（Westley）童話冒險故事。美麗的牛奶杯公主認為自己比農場男孩衛斯理高貴許多，因此總是以瞧不起的姿態對待他。每次牛奶杯公主對他下命令時，他總是回答「如你所願」。後來她終於明白衛斯理的「如你所願」實際上是在說「我愛你」，她也一樣愛著他。兩人互許終生，但衛斯理決定他必須離開小鎮出海去尋找財富，他答應她，會回來娶她為妻。然而，衛斯理的船受到可怕的羅伯茲海盜（the Dread Pirate Roberts）攻擊，衛斯理被認為應該死了。五年之後，牛奶杯公主同意嫁給漢伯丁克王子（Prince Humperdinck），即便她並不愛他。然而，她在婚禮前被壞人綁架了。歷經一段危險旅程之後，她被一個黑衣男子拯救，她覺得這男子應該就是可怕的羅伯茲海盜本人。她跟海盜坦承自己並不愛漢伯丁克王子，同時跟他說，希望他去死因為他殺了自己心愛的男人。說完便將他推下山坡。當他滾下山的同時大喊著「如你所願」時，她立刻意識他，原來這男子是衛斯理！

Return to the World of Wonderland

The Giant is sitting in the basket attached to the front of Tim's bike. They are riding to the Wizard's mansion as fast as they can. Some of Tim's 'Essence of Rainbow' magic powder begins trickling out from his backpack and Tim notices his bike is now flying through the sky. He continues peddling the bike as they pass in front of the moon before they land successfully in front of the Wizard's house.

Act Seven Scene 1

In the Wizard's mansion.

Tim — Why did the Wolf kidnap the Three Little Pigs?

Wizard — The new Mouse King is planning to wage a war against people in the World of Wonderland. He needs the pigs to show him the interior structure of the King's castle.

The Wizard tells Tim the story to explain why the new Mouse King wants revenge for his father's death, as well as how his requests for forgiveness were in vain.

Tim — Is there anything we can do to prevent war? The fairy tale world is supposed to have happily-ever-after endings.

Wizard — You are such a romantic dreamer! The World of Wonderland is just like your world. There are all kinds of people. Some are kind, some are evil, and some are just plainly hateful...

Tim — I know but I'm not the only dreamer... .

Giant *(pointing at himself)* Yeah, someone like me dreams of turning back into a GIANT!

Tim Oh, this is my friend, the Giant.

Giant Nice to meet you, Mr. Wizard. Can we have some of your magical flour, so I can undo the spell?

Wizard Tell me first, what can you do for the World of Wonderland?

Giant Errr... Once I am giant again, I can easily destroy a whole mouse army with a snap of my finger. Oh, I can give you my word that I won't eat much of the food supply during the battle.

Wizard Fair enough. But I am out of magical flour, I will have to give it to you later.

Giant Thank you sir!

Wizard *(checking his watch)* Oh, it's time to text my girlfriend so that she knows I'm home!

Tim is shocked when he sees the online dating profile photo displayed on the Wizard's iPad.

Tim — That's the profile of Snow White's stepmother!

Wizard — Why do you say that?

Tim — Because I helped set-up that profile for her.

Wizard — This must be a coincidence. My girlfriend is NOT THE QUEEN!

Tim — Calm down Romeo, it's no big deal!

Giant — (*chuckling*) If Tim is right, I'm going to get a kick out of it when you two meet.

第七幕

重返魔幻世界

　　巨人坐在提姆的腳踏車前面的籃子裡，他們盡全速要趕到巫師的莊園，提姆背包裡的一些彩虹元素魔法粉末開始灑落下來，他注意到他的腳踏車飛上天，當他們越過掛在天上的月亮時，提姆持續地踩著腳踏車的踏板，最後成功地在巫師家門口降落。

在巫師的莊園

提姆 ▸ 為什麼野狼要綁架三隻小豬？

巫師 ▸ 新鼠王計畫向魔幻世界的人類宣戰，他需要豬仔告訴他國王城堡建築的內部結構。
巫師告訴提姆為何新鼠王想要為他父王復仇的故事，以及他一再請求原諒卻沒用。

提姆 ▸ 我們可以做什麼來阻止戰爭呢？童話故事的世界應該是要走「從此過著幸福快樂的生活」這種結局。

巫師 ▸ 你真是個浪漫的夢想家！魔幻世界和你的世界一樣，有各式各樣的人，有些人心地善良，有些人很邪惡，還有些人徹底的令人討厭。

提姆 ▸ 我知道，但我不是唯一一個愛做夢的人啊…

巨人 ▸ （指著自己）也是，像我就一直夢想著重回巨人的樣子。

提姆 ▸ 喔對了，這是我的朋友，巨人。

巨人 ▸ 巫師先生，很高興認識你，你可以給我一些你的魔法麵粉，讓我解除咒語嗎？

巫師 ▸ 先告訴我，你能為魔幻世界做什麼？

巨人 ▶ 哦⋯我一旦恢復成巨人就可以輕易地在彈指之間摧毀掉整個老鼠大軍，喔⋯我也向你保證，在戰爭期間，我不會吃太多補給品的。

巫師 ▶ 聽起來還算是合理的提議，不過魔法麵粉剛好沒了，我晚點才能給你。

巨人 ▶ 謝謝你。

巫師 ▶ （看了一下他的手錶）喔，我該傳簡訊給我的女朋友，讓她知道我回到家了。
當提姆看到巫師的 iPad 上的線上交友大頭照時，感到非常震驚。

提姆 ▶ 那是白雪公主的繼母！

巫師 ▶ 你為什麼知道呢？

提姆 ▶ 因為我幫她建立檔案啊。

巫師 ▶ 這一定是巧合，我的女朋友才不是皇后！

提姆 ▶ 冷靜一下，羅密歐，這沒什麼大不了的！

巨人 ▶ （呵呵笑）如果提姆是對的話，當你們兩個見面時，我一定會笑到不行。

Phrases & Sentence Patterns 慣用語 & 句型

❶ wage a war against 對⋯宣戰

❷ as well（as）也；和

❸ a snap of my finger 彈指之間

❹ give you my word 向你保證

❺ fair enough 行；還算合理的，我同意

❻ calm down 冷靜

❼ It's no big deal！沒什麼大不了的！別大驚小怪！

❽ get a kick out of something 某事好笑有趣

Cultural Note

In this story, the Wizard calls Tim a dreamer and describes the fact that the World of Wonderland is composed of both good and bad people. Has the Wizard's statement reminded you of the song Imagine by John Lennon, one of the members of the Beatles? Imagine describes a world where people live life in peace without being killed or dying because of the hatred between two countries or religions. He sings about sharing everything by giving up material possessions so that greed or hunger can be eliminated. It is difficult to create a world like this, as referenced in the lyrics that say, "You may say I'm a dreamer/But I'm not the only one". Sadly, on December 8, 1980, John Lennon was murdered outside The Dakota apartment building, which is across from Central

Park in New York City. To remember the English rock star, Central Park has a Strawberry Fields memorial with The Dakota in the background that is dedicated to John Lennon. There you will see the word "Imagine" on the memorial mosaic.

文化角落

　　在故事裡，巫師說提姆是一個愛做夢的人，並告訴提姆一個事實，也就是魔幻世界同時包含好人與壞人。巫師的一番話有沒有讓你想起披頭四約翰藍儂的一首歌《想像》呢？《想像》這首歌描述一個人們和平相處的世界，沒有因為國與國之間或是區域之間的怨恨而造成的殺戮或死亡。他所唱的世界，所有人拋棄對物質的佔有，所有事物皆共享，因此貪婪或是飢餓可以被消滅。就像歌詞裡說的，要實現這樣的世界很困難：「你可以說我是一個愛做夢的人／但我絕不是唯一的一個。」令人傷心的是，1980 年 12 月 8 日當天，約翰藍儂在達可塔公寓（*Dakota apartment building*）外面被謀殺了，這公寓就在紐約中央公園的對面。為了紀念這位英國搖滾樂手，中央公園裡，以達可塔公寓為背景的那面，蓋了一座草莓園紀念館獻給約翰藍儂。在那裡你還可以找到「想像」這一個字刻畫在有馬賽克花樣的紀念碑上面。

The Wizard spends the next 10 minutes texting his girlfriend while Tim and the Giant are playing online chess. After texting, the Wizard is smiling with a look of happiness.

Wizard　Sorry for the digression. Let me video conference with King Stylish, so I can introduce you to him.

Tim　King Stylish?

Wizard　Yes. He is my best friend in the World of Wonderland. We used to sneak out together to Chicago and tailgate before football games.

Tim　Stay on topic, please!

Wizard　Ok. In short, King Stylish will be the new Mouse King's target.

The Wizard opens an online video conferencing room and invites King Stylish to join the meeting.

Wizard ► Greetings, Your Majesty. This is Tim BeauDaring whom I mentioned to you before.

Tim ► (*bowing*) It is nice to meet you, Your Majesty.

King Stylish ► Nice to meet you, Tim. You look younger and smaller than I expected. However, a great warrior is not judged by his age and stature.

Giant ► (*proudly pounding his chest*) I see eye to eye with you, Your Majesty!

Tim ► (*pointing to the Giant*) This is my sidekick, the Giant.

King Stylish ► Very well. Please return to the World of Wonderland as soon as possible. We have to come up with a defensive strategy. Wizard, please stay in your world and prepare for a war.

The Wizard smiles and then bows to show his agreement. The video conferencing ends.

Wizard ► Tim, go pack things you think might be useful for this journey. Then I will send you back to the

World of Wonderland.

Tim ▸ I think I'll be grounded forever if my parents find out I'm going somewhere they don't know for... probably several days.

Wizard ▸ No worries. I chatted with your parents earlier. I've got you covered.

　　巫師花了接下來的 10 分鐘和他的女朋友傳簡訊，提姆和巨人則在下線上西洋棋，傳完簡訊之後，巫師微笑並露出滿臉幸福的表情。

巫師 ▸ 真不好意思離題了，我來開視訊和時尚王通話，介紹你和他認識。

提姆 ▸ 時尚王？

巫師 ▸ 是的，他是我在魔幻世界最好的朋友，我們曾經一起偷溜到芝加哥參加橄欖球賽的車隊派對。

提姆 ▸ 拜託，別岔題！

巫師 ▸ 好，簡言之，時尚王將是新鼠王的目標。
　　巫師開了一間線上視訊會議室，並邀請時尚王加入會議。

Act Seven Scene 2

巫師 ▶ 國王陛下您好，這是我之前跟你提過的提姆・博德林（Tim BeauDaring）。

提姆 ▶ （鞠躬）國王陛下，很高興認識您。

時尚王 ▶ 提姆，很高興認識你，你看起來比我預期的年輕，個頭也不大，不過，一個優秀的勇士是不能以他的年齡與身材做判斷的。

巨人 ▶ （驕傲地拍打自己的胸膛）國王陛下，我們真是英雄所見略同。

提姆 ▶ （指著巨人）巨人是我的副手。

時尚王 ▶ 非常好，請盡速回到魔幻世界，我們得策劃防守策略。巫師，還煩請你待在那世界準備迎戰。
巫師微笑點頭表示同意。視訊會議結束。

巫師 ▶ 提姆，快去打包你認為在這趟旅行可能會派上用場的東西，然後我會送你們回魔幻世界。

提姆 ▶ 我想，如果我爸媽發現我去一個他們不清楚的地方…還可能好幾天，我會被禁足一輩子吧。

巫師 ▶ 別擔心，我稍早之前已經和他們聊過了，已經搞定了。

Phrases & Sentence Patterns慣用語 & 句型

❶ with a look of +（表示心情的）名詞：帶著一臉…表情
❷ sneak out 偷溜走

❸ Stay on topic. 別離題

❹ in short 簡言之

❺ see eye to eye with someone 有相同的看法

❻ come up with 想出

❼ be grounded 被禁足

❽ I've got you covered. 我幫你都打點好了；我罩你；我掩護你

Cultural Note

The word "tailgate" as a noun means the hinged door at the back of a truck, while as a verb it means a vehicle driving too close behind another. You can complain, "That car is tailgating me! That's annoying." When it comes to sports, the word "tailgate" is referring to a particular kind of party held during the sport seasons. At a tailgating party, many pick-up trucks are gathered together in a big parking lot or open area. Traditionally, people wear clothes in their team's colors to show their support. Decorative items such as flags and stickers are also popular. People eat a lot of food cooked on small grills, consume a large quantity of adult drinks, and play games to celebrate the sporting event. Beer is always one of the essential elements at a tailgating party. There are games themed around drinking beer as well. However, you should be

Part 2
Return to the World of Wonderland

careful! In most areas, you are not allowed to carry around an open alcoholic beverage. The police could give you a ticket!

文化角落

　　英文字 *tailgate* 當名詞時的意思是貨車／卡車尾的門，當動詞的意思是後面車輛緊隨前面的車輛行駛。你可以抱怨說「後面那部車跟太緊了，真討厭。」當提到運動時，*tailgate* 這個字指在球季時所舉辦的特別派對。舉辦車隊派對（*tailgating party*）時,很多小型卡車（後面是開放可載物的貨車）會聚在一個大停車場或是開放空間。傳統上，大家會穿著所支持的球隊顏色的衣服，以示支持，一些裝飾用品像是旗子和貼紙也很受歡迎，大家會一起吃用小型烤肉架烤的食物，喝很多含酒精飲料，然後一起玩遊戲慶祝球季盛事。啤酒一向是車隊派對不可或缺的東西，很多的遊戲都圍繞著喝啤酒這主題。不過，要小心！大部份的地方是不允許帶著已開瓶的含酒精飲料在路上行走。警察看到是會開罰單的！

Tim and the Giant return to the Wizard's mansion, both carrying a gigantic backpack.

Wizard (*amused with what he sees*) I assume that you both know that you're NOT traveling to the World of Wonderland for fun as a backpacker, right?

Tim (*nodding*) I'm very professional! My backpack is loaded with hi-tech gadgets.

Giant Oops. I am just a backpacker going back home... with a lot of souvenirs!

The Wizard leads them to the location of the world traveling portal.

Tim This looks like a regular door to a storage room.

Wizard Never judge a door by its appearance! (*He tries to pull the door open, but can't.*)

Tim Very true. It doesn't look like a broken door until

you try to open it. Let the future great wizard try! (*He raises both of his arms and wiggles his fingers at the door*.) Open sesame!!

Wizard — Stop goofing around! (*He grabs his toolbox*.) I think the doorknob is jammed, let me fix it.

Tim — Why don't you use your magic to get it fixed?

Wizard — Nope, I want to be handy at fixing things!

Tim — You sound so much like my dad.

While waiting for the Wizard to fix the doorknob, Tim and the Giant become so bored that they start to play an online roleplaying game together. A half hour later, the Wizard is all sweaty but proudly announces the door is fixed.

Wizard — The Ta da!!

Tim — (*shaking his head when looking inside the door*) Err... everything is upside down.

Giant — Yep. I see trees above my head and birds flying under my feet.

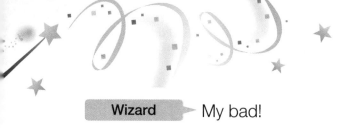

Wizard ► My bad!

The Wizard closes the door and makes a couple of adjustments. Tim opens the door again.

Tim ► Great job! It looks normal now.

Wizard ► Alright, have a safe and fun trip!

The Wizard pushes both Tim and the Giant into the World of Wonderland. As soon as Tim and the Giant are gone, the Wizard wraps a small note around his Golden Bird's leg and whispers something to her. She nods and flies away.

Wizard ► (*mumbling to himself*) Fingers crossed. I hope Tim can stop the new Mouse King's plan.

 第三場

提姆和巨人雙雙背著一個巨大的後背包回到巫師的莊園。

巫師 ► （對於眼前所見到的景象感到很有趣）我想你們兩個都知道，這趟去魔幻世界不是只當個去玩樂的背包客吧？

提姆 ► （點頭）我很專業的！我的背包裡裝滿一堆高科技小玩意。

巨人 ▶ 阿喔，我只是一個要回家的背包客…裡面一堆紀念品！
巫師帶他們到穿越不同世界入口的地點。

提姆 ▶ 這看起很像一般儲藏室的門。

巫師 ▶ 不要以貌取「門」！（他試著拉開門但拉不開。）

提姆 ▶ 你説得對，看起來不像壞掉的門直到你試著打開它，讓未來的偉大巫師試看看吧！（他舉起雙手並揮動他的手指頭）芝麻開門！

巫師 ▶ 別搞笑了！（他拿來他的工具箱）我想門把卡住了，我修看看。

提姆 ▶ 你為什麼不用你的魔法修呢？

巫師 ▶ 不想，我也要當一個很會修東西的人！

提姆 ▶ 你聽起來超像我老爸。
當提姆和巨人在等巫師修理門把的同時，他們覺得無聊，於是開始玩起線上角色扮演的遊戲，半小時之後，巫師雖然滿身是汗，但很自豪地宣布門修好了。

巫師 ▶ 鏘鏘！

提姆 ▶ （當他往門裡探的時候搖搖頭）這…所有東西的上下顛倒了耶。

巨人 ▶ 是啊，我看到樹在我頭頂，鳥在我腳底飛。

巫師　　真不好意思！
　　巫師關上門在做了一點調整，提姆再度把門打開。

提姆　　幹得好啊！現在看起來是正常的了。

巫師　　好極了，祝有個安全愉快的旅程！
　　巫師一把將提姆和巨人推向魔幻世界去，他們走之後，巫師將一小張紙條綁在他的金色小鳥腳上，並輕聲交待一些話，她點點頭就飛走了。

巫師　　（自言自語）祝我們好運，但願提姆可以阻止新鼠王的計畫。

Phrases & Sentence Patterns慣用語 & 句型

❶ be loaded with 裝滿…

❷ Never judge a door by its appearance.（改編自 "Never judge people by their appearance." 別以貌取人）

❸ goof around 別鬧了，正經一點

❹ be handy at 手巧的

❺ upside down 上下顛倒

❻ my bad 對不起；不好意思 （非正式地表示抱歉，承認自己做錯什麼，通常用的時機是對方是你熟識的人。）

❼ Have a safe and fun trip. 祝有個安全愉快的旅程

❽ Fingers crossed. 祝好運

Cultural Note

If women are always missing one piece of clothes in her closet, men in the U.S. probably always want one more tool for his home improvement projects. It might be a slight exaggeration to make such a statement. However, it is true that Americans tend to have all kinds of tools for fixing things. One reason is that labor is expensive in the U.S. For example, it can cost more than US $100 just to have someone come to your place simply to EXAMINE a clogged drain. Then, you would need to make another appointment to fix the issue and, of course, pay them more money! Although financial considerations might be one reason for the American man's tool obsession, it is not the only one. In fact, many people do enjoy spending their leisure time making over their houses. It is common to see friends proudly posting the before and after pictures of a new look to their house on Facebook.

　　若說女人的衣櫥永遠少一件衣服，美國的男人可能永遠都需要另一樣工具讓他進行家庭改造計畫。這樣說或許有點誇張，不過美國人的確傾向擁有各式各樣可以修東西的工具。一個理由是美國的勞工很貴。舉例來說，光請人到家裡單單檢查一下堵住的排水管就可能會花上你至少美金 100 大洋。然後你還得額外預約時間請人來將問題解決，當然囉，肯定要再付一筆錢！雖然財務考量可以用來解釋美國男人對於工具著迷的原因，但卻不是唯一的原因。實際上，很多人的休閒嗜好就是改造他們的家，所以，可以常常看到朋友的臉書上，很自豪地的放上家裡裝修前與裝修後新模樣的照片。

Scene 4 ⭐ 🎧 MP3 33

During the ride to the World of Wonderland, Tim sees several windows ahead. He chooses the one where Snow White is about to bite into an apple. Tim and the Giant fall into the Seven Dwarfs' house.

Snow White   My goodness. I almost choked because of your sudden fall from the sky.

Tim   On the contrary, I just SAVED YOU from choking on that apple. Why do you like apples so much anyway?

Snow White   My father always tells me, "An apple a day keeps the doctor away."

The Peasant Wife   (*talking from outside the door*) That's right. Apples are healthy!

Tim   Take my advice! It is more practical to remember, "An apple a day keeps anyone away if you throw it hard enough."

Snow White   Hahaha! You're funny! But I'll never throw an

apple at anybody.

Tim — For your safety, you shouldn't eat apples from strangers.

Snow White — Why not? She seems like a very nice lady.

Tim — Hmmm... because... apples can have some harmful pesticides! *(He searches for the fruits with the most pesticides on his iPad to show her.)* See! Apples are in the list of the top ten most toxic fruits and vegetables.

Snow White — Oh my, that is very informative. Point taken! I will wash and peel my apples from now on.

The Peasant Wife — My dear, please try just one bite of my delicious apple and tell me if you like it. This apple is organic!!

Snow White — *(suddenly losing interest in apples)* Sorry, I have changed my mind. Bye.

Tim looks around the house for the Giant and finds him using the oven to heat up the Chicago pizza he brought back.

Tim　(*talking to the Peasant Wife*) Err... I think she's looking forward to something cheesy now.

The Peasant Wife　(*grunting in frustration*) Ahh... fine! I'll see you around.

第四場

　　到魔幻世界的途中，提姆看到眼前有一些不同的窗口，他選了白雪公主正要咬下蘋果的那扇窗。提姆和巨人便掉落在七個小矮人家裡的地板上。

白雪公主　我的天啊，因為你們忽然從天而降，我差點嗆到。

提姆　正好相反，我剛拯救了你，讓你沒被蘋果嗆到。對了，你為什麼這麼喜歡吃蘋果呢？

白雪公主　我父王總是跟我說「每日一蘋果，身體健康，醫生不來找」。

村婦　（在門外說）這就對了，蘋果很健康的！

提姆　採納一下我的意見！比較實際的說法是「每日一蘋果，丟得夠大力時，麻煩人物不來找」。

白雪公主　哈哈哈！你真有趣！可是我絕對不可能對任何人丟蘋果的。

提姆 ▶ 為了你的安全，你不應該吃陌生人給你的蘋果。

白雪公主 ▶ 為什麼不可以？她看起來像是非常不錯的女士。

提姆 ▶ 恩…因為…蘋果會有一些有害的殺蟲劑！（他用他的 iPad 搜尋殘留最多殺蟲劑的水果給她看）你看！蘋果在最毒的蔬果裡名列前十。

白雪公主 ▶ 天啊，真是受教了，記得了！我會從現在起都洗蘋果，削蘋果皮的。

村婦 ▶ 親愛的，請就試一口我那好吃的蘋果，然後告訴我你喜不喜歡，這蘋果是有機的！！

白雪公主 ▶ （忽然對蘋果失去興趣）抱歉，我改變心意了，掰。
提姆環顧房子四周在找巨人，發現他在用烤箱加熱帶回來的芝加哥披薩。

提姆 ▶ （對著村婦說）恩…我想她現在正在期待起司味十足的東西。

村婦 ▶ （感到很沮喪地哼了一聲）啊…算了！我們回頭見。

Phrases & Sentence Patterns 慣用語 & 句型

❶ on the contrary 恰好相反

❷ An apple a day keeps the doctor away. 每日一蘋果，身體健康，醫生不來找。

❸ take one's advice 接受意見

❹ point taken：接受（常用來表示接受某人所說的觀點）

❺ heat up 加熱（食物）

❻ look forward to + 名詞或動名詞：期待

❼ cheesy 多起司的（註：但 cheesy 另一意是「老套的」，所以一語雙關暗示白雪公主的喜好，例如老套的追求方式等）

❽ I'll see you around. 再見（= See you later.）

Cultural Note

The first thing that comes to people's minds when thinking about New York City is the hot tourist spots, such as The Empire State Building, The Statue of Liberty, Time Square, Broadway shows, and so on. Fruit production is likely to be the last thing people think of. However, according to USDA National Agricultural Statistics Service, New York State is the second-largest apple producing state in the country behind Washington State. Although, if you think New York City's nickname "Big Apple" came from its fruit production you'd be wrong. There have been many claims on the Internet and elsewhere about where the nickname "Big Apple" came from. One thing in common in these claims is that the nickname has nothing to do with New York State's apple production! If you ever have an opportunity to join a local tour in New York, it would be *interesting to ask the tourist guides. Maybe each tourist guide will give you a different version of the story!*

文化角落

　　一想到紐約時，大家想到的第一件事就是旅遊熱門景點，像是帝國大廈、自由女神像、時代廣場、百老匯表演等。水果生產可能是最不會讓人聯想到的。不過，根據美國農業統計服務（USDA National Agricultural Statistics Service），紐約州是全美第二大蘋果生產地，僅次於華盛頓州。若你因此覺得紐約的暱稱「大蘋果」是來自水果生產的話，那可就錯了。網路上和其他來源對於「大蘋果」這暱稱的來源有很多辯論，但有一個共通點是，絕對和蘋果生產沒關係！如果你有機會去紐約，並跟著當地導遊觀光，可以問一問導遊這個問題，或許每個導遊都會給你不同版本的故事！

Scene 5  MP3 34

As Snow White and the Giant are eating the Chicago pizza, Tim is setting up his GPS to guide them to King Stylish's castle.

Tim — Alright, we'd better go!

Giant — Can I stay here?

Tim — Nope! You promised to be my sidekick.

Snow White — (*chuckling*) I'll take care of the rest of the pizza for you.

Tim — (*putting a headlamp on the Giant*) Cheer up! I'll let you lead the way with this magic torch!

Giant — (*moving his head left to right several times*) This is cool! The light goes wherever my head moves.

With the help of the GPS and the headlamp, Tim and the Giant arrive at the castle by sunrise.

King Stylish ➤ Welcome Tim. It is nice to finally meet you in person.

Tim ➤ It's nice to meet you too, Your Majesty.

Giant ➤ Your Majesty, have you ever held a parade to show off your new clothes to your people... only to find that you ended up wearing an undershirt and boxers?
The guards quickly seize the Giant.

Tim ➤ Please forgive him, Your Majesty!

King Stylish ➤ (*waving at the guards to let go of the Giant*) No worries. I've learned my lesson and won't allow people to pull invisible clothes over my eyes again.

As King Stylish is getting up from his seat to lead them to the conference room, he starts to have an upset stomach. After several visits to the restroom, King Stylish feels faint and weak. Unfortunately, the doctor is away on leave. Tim offers to help check the King's condition.

Tim ➤ (*checking the King's temperature with a digital*

thermometer) Good news. You don't have a fever. (*He takes out his smartphone and opens the health app.*) Please put one finger over this camera eye and hold still. I'm going to check your heartrate. (*He announces happily.*) Your pulse is perfect. I think you must have just eaten something bad that has irritated your bowel this morning.

King Stylish ▶ I must get better soon. The meeting for combat preparation will be held this afternoon.

Tim ▶ I got some over-the-counter medication with me that might help you.

After taking the medication and getting some rest, the King finally feels better.

第五場

　　當白雪公主和巨人在吃芝加哥披薩的時候，提姆正在設定前往時尚王城堡的衛星導航路線。

提姆 ▶ 好了，我們最好出發了！

巨人 ▶ 我可以待在這裡嗎？

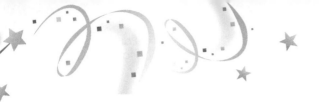

提姆　不行！你答應要當我的副手的。

白雪公主　（呵呵笑）我會幫你吃完剩下的披薩的。

提姆　（將一個頭燈戴在巨人頭上）開心一點！這次我讓你用這魔法火把帶路！

巨人　（將頭左右擺動好幾次）太酷了！這燈會跟著我的頭移動耶。
因為衛星導航和頭燈的幫忙，提姆和巨人在日出前順利抵達城堡。

時尚王　提姆，歡迎你，終於見到你本人了。

提姆　我也很高興見到您，國王殿下。

巨人　國王陛下，您是否曾經舉辦遊行，向人民炫耀您的新衣服…到最後發現，自己只穿了一件內衣和四角褲呢？
侍衛迅速地將巨人抓起來。

提姆　國王陛下，請原諒他！

時尚王　（揮手讓侍衛放了巨人）別擔心，我已學到教訓了，不會再讓人用看不見的衣服蒙蔽我的雙眼（暗喻：被欺騙，被耍）。
當時尚王正要從座位起身帶他們去會議室時，他開始感到肚子痛，跑了幾次廁所之後，時尚王感到又暈又虛弱。不幸地是，御醫正好放假不在身邊，提姆提出要幫忙看一下國王的狀況。

提姆　（用數位溫度計量了一下國王的體溫）好消息，您沒有發燒。（他拿出他的智慧型手機，並且打開健康應用程式）現在請您將手指放在鏡頭這裡，並且保持不動，我要量一下您的心跳。（他開心地宣布）您的脈搏很完美，我想您一定只是今天早上吃了不好的東西，才讓肚子不舒服。

時尚王　我必須趕快好起來，今天下午還要召開作戰準備會議。

提姆　我帶了一些成藥在身上，或許可以幫助您。
　　　吃了藥，休息了一會兒，時尚王終於覺得好多了。

Phrases & Sentence Patterns慣用語 & 句型

❶ take care of 處理；負責

❷ Cheer up！振作起來！高興起來！

❸ learn one's lesson 學到教訓

❹ pull the invisible clothes over my eyes，改編自 "pull the wool over your eyes" 比喻「被欺騙」、「被耍」

❺ have a upset stomach 肚子不舒服

❻ on leave 休假

❼ have a fever 發燒

❽ over-the-counter（藥品）非處方的，無需處方也可買到的

In Hans Christian Andersen's "The Emperor's New Clothes," the two liars promise to weave the most magnificent clothes for the Emperor. However, only those who are fit for their position can see the clothes. Since no one, including the Emperor, wants to appear unfit for their position, they all pretend to see the non-existent fabric. It is not until the parade when an innocent and honest boy shouts, "The Emperor hasn't got anything on" do people start to realize they are all fooled. An English expression "honest to a fault" can be pertinent to this situation. Although honesty is considered a virtue, sometimes an honest comment can hurt people's feelings or embarrass them. This is how being honest becomes a "fault" in one's personality. Many American sit-coms use this element to create a comic effect because, people, especially adults, are not supposed to mention things like a person's weight gain. For example, it will embarrass your friend if you greet him/her with a joke by saying "Looks like marriage life has caused you to put on some weight, right?" Weight gain is just simply a taboo topic no matter what.

Act **Seven** Scene 5

文化角落

　　安徒生童話故事《國王的新衣》裡，有兩個騙子答應國王將會做一件富麗堂皇的衣服給他穿，不過唯有適任其職位的人才看得到這件衣服。因為沒有人願意讓人覺得自己不適任，包括國王他自己，所以大家都假裝看得見這件不存在的布料。一直到遊行那天，有個天真誠實的小男孩大叫「國王什麼都沒穿」時，人們才開始意識到自己被耍了。不過，雖然誠實是美德，有時候太過誠實的評論也可能會傷害一個人的情感或讓他感到尷尬。英文上來說即是，個性上太誠實到變成了一個「缺點」。許多美國的情境喜劇就是利用這元素來創造娛樂效果，因為有些事是不該被提及的，尤其是在成人的世界裡，像是當某人變胖的時候，譬如，如果你向你的朋友打招呼時，開的玩笑是「看來婚姻生活讓你增胖了一些，對吧？」你的朋友可能會感到尷尬。無論如何，變胖這話題純粹是一個禁忌。

In the afternoon, a combat preparation conference is held. The King's Knights, Tim and the Giant are all summoned.

King Stylish — The annual summer carnival begins tomorrow. It is our tradition to hold a Masquerade Ball on the first evening.

Tim — The ball will be perfect timing for an invasion.

King Stylish — A penny for your thoughts?

Tim — Since they have the Three Little Pigs, I think they might try to enter the castle through the secret tunnels.

King Stylish — I'll have guards watching those tunnels closely.

The Knights in the conference room all agree and nod.

Giant — Your Majesty, you can also try grilling some sweet corn at different locations. The Three Little Pigs can't resist!

King Stylish — Excellent idea!

Giant — *(feeling on top of the world)* Thanks for the compliment, Your Majesty!

King Stylish — The Witch of the Candy House is in charge of catering. We'll make sure she prepares some ears of corn.

Tim — It just came to me... I have some baby monitors that can be useful. We can monitor the ballroom from another room!

Giant — We? Do you mean you and I?

Tim — Aren't you my sidekick?

Giant — (reluctantly) Ye-e-eah. But... I'm looking forward to the Masquerade Ball.

Tim — Ok, you can stay in the ballroom. (*He gives the Giant a wristwatch walkie-talkie.*) Put this on and be sure you contact me every half hour.

King Stylish Great! (*He shows Tim his handheld device.*) Oh, the Wizard gave me this for video conferencing. Can we use it too?

Tim Of course. We should also ask every guest to take a selfie and tag themselves on Facebook when they enter the ball. Then we can create a database of all the party guests!

King Stylish Excellent! This way we can efficiently identify the enemies. What do you think of all these plans so far, Tim?

Tim All sounds good to me! But the ball is in your court, Your Majesty!

King Stylish Alright, I think we're all set for the battle! Let the show begin!

下午召開作戰準備會議，國王的騎士，提姆和巨人都被召喚過去。

時尚王 明天就開始一年一度的夏日嘉年華會，根據傳統，化裝舞會將在第一個夜晚舉行。

提姆　舞會將是完美的入侵時機。

時尚王　有任何想法嗎？

提姆　既然他們抓了三隻小豬，我想他們可能會從秘密通道進入城堡。

時尚王　我會讓守衛緊緊看好那些通道的。
所有在會議室的騎士都點頭同意。

巨人　國王陛下，您也可以試著在不同地點烤一些甜玉米，三隻小豬很難抗拒的！

時尚王　太棒的主意了！

巨人　（感到自豪得意）謝謝國王陛下的讚美！

時尚王　糖果屋的巫婆負責外燴，我們會請她務必準備一些玉米。

提姆　我忽然想到⋯我有一些嬰兒監視器可以派上用場，我們可以從另一個房間監視舞會的情況！

巨人　我們？你指的是我和你嗎？

提姆　你不是我的副手嗎？

巨人　（不情願地）是⋯啦，可是⋯我很期待這化裝舞會。

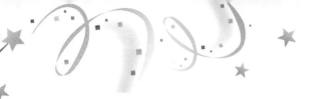

提姆 ▶ 好啦，你可以待在舞廳（他給巨人一個手腕型對講機）你將這個帶上，一定要每半小時跟我回報。

時尚王 ▶ 好極了！（他給提姆看自己的掌上型電子裝備）喔，巫師給我這個和他視訊，我們也可以拿來用嗎？

提姆 ▶ 當然可以，我們也應該請每位客人在進來舞廳時都拍一張自拍照，然後在臉書上標註自己，這樣我們就可以建立舞會當天客人的資料檔案了！

時尚王 ▶ 太棒了！如此一來，我們可以很有效率地找出誰是敵人。提姆，你覺得目前所有的計畫聽起來如何呢？

提姆 ▶ 我覺得都很棒！不過，場子是國王陛下您的，由您發球下決定！

時尚王 ▶ 很好，我想我們已經準備好迎戰了！讓好戲上場吧！

Phrases & Sentence Patterns慣用語 & 句型

❶ a penny for your thoughts 你怎麼想的？告訴我你的想法。

❷ on top of the world 感到非常開心；感到非常幸福；感到非常自豪

❸ in charge of 負責

❹ come to somebody 忽然想到什麼想法或想起什麼

❺ take a selfie 自拍

❻ The ball is in your court. 由你決定

❼ be all set 準備好了

❽ Let the show begin. 讓好戲上場吧

Cultural Note

In the story, the Mouse King says that life throws him a curve ball. Later, Tim tells King Stylish that "the ball is in your court", so the king should make the decision. In English, there are many other idioms using a 'ball' as metaphor. Another common idiom is "on the ball," which is used to describe people who are competent and knowledgeable. Without surprise, the origin of the saying "on the ball" is associated with sports. The saying originated in British football (or soccer) but became more prevalent as other games involving balls became popular. In addition to referring to sports, a "ball" can be a formal social gathering for dancing. Another saying "have a ball" means to have an exciting time. For example, your friends plan to go to a tropical island for a vacation. They may be excited to tell you that, "I'm going to have a ball while I'm on vacation!" Finally, let's end this discussion with the expression "a real goofball." When you have done something silly or acted like a fool, your parents may chuckle and say, "you are a real goofball!"

　　在本故事中，老鼠王説，「生命丟給他一個變化球」。後來提姆跟時尚王説，「球在你的庭上」，決定權在國王手上。英文裡有很多諺語都拿球來當比喻。另一個常聽到的諺語是 *on the ball*，用來形容一個人很有競爭力且懂很多。令人一點都不感到訝異的是，這諺語源自英國足球，而且當其他球類運動也流行起來時，這諺語逐漸變得很盛行。*Ball* 這英文字除了當「球類」一意解釋之外，也可以當「正式社交聚會的舞會」解釋，所以另一個諺語 *have a ball*，意思是「令人感到興奮的時刻。」例如，你的朋友正計劃前往熱帶島嶼度假，他們可能情緒高昂地跟你説「旅行時，我要玩得很嗨很開心！」最後，讓我們以 *a real goofball* 結束這單元。當你幹了什麼蠢事或是行為像個笨蛋時，你的父母可能會笑你並説「你真的很搞笑耶！」

Scene 1

Back in the Mouse King's castle, the new Mouse King is holding a meeting with his minions.

New Mouse King   Tomorrow is going to be a historical victory for us!

The Wolf   Hoowooooo!

New Mouse King   King Stylish is skilled at defense, so we'll have to keep him off balance.

The Wolf   *(feeling excited)* I love to tease my prey before eating them!

New Mouse King   Since everyone will be dressed up for the Masquerade Ball, we need to find King Stylish and seize him first.

The Wolf That should be easy! He made a fool of himself at that parade last year. I can recognize him by the mole on his back!

New Mouse King That was really one of the worst scandals a king could've had. I hope that he'll put more clothes on this time. Hahaha!

The mouse guards bring up the Three Little Pigs.

New Mouse King How were my men treating you in the dungeon?

Three Little Pigs Very well, Your Mousety.

New Mouse King Tomorrow, each one of you will lead a team into the castle through the secret tunnels. After you successfully enter the castle, you've got my word that all pigs in the World of Wonderland will have freedom from the fear of being attacked by wolves.

The Wolf (*protesting loudly*) What about your all-you-can-eat promise to me?

New Mouse King — (*winking at the Wolf*) Well, I only promised all pigs in the World of Wonderland would be safe from wolves. Once I conquer the world the little boy comes from, you can have all the smoked pig you want, a.k.a. bacon. How does that sound to you?

The Wolf — Sounds delicious!

Third Little Pig — (*trying to digress from the uncomfortable conversation*)
What if King Stylish's guards are waiting in the tunnels to ambush us?

New Mouse King — Remember, do not continue fighting until your last breath! Surrender immediately so they think they are safe!

The Wolf — (*smirking*) We'll wait for them to think they're out of immediate danger. Then we'll attack when they least expect it!

New Mouse King — Shall we all put our costumes on now? We have a Masquerade Ball to attend!

The Wolf Absolutely.

第八幕
復仇

第一場

回到鼠王的城堡，新鼠王正在和他的爪牙們開會。

新鼠王 明天將是迎接我們歷史性勝利的一刻！

野狼 嚎～嗚～！

新鼠王 時尚王擅於防守，所以我們要攻其不備。

野狼 （感到非常興奮）我喜歡在吃掉獵物之前玩弄一下他們！

新鼠王 既然每個人都盛裝打扮去參加化裝舞會，我們得找到時尚王，先擒王。

野狼 那應該不成問題！他去年在遊行上出糗，我現在連他背上的痣都能認得了！

新鼠王 那還真是一國之君可以鬧出來的最糟的醜聞，希望這次他能多穿幾件衣服在身上，哈哈哈！
鼠衛將三隻小豬帶上來。

新鼠王 ▸ 在地窖的人待你們如何呢？

三隻小豬 ▸ 非常好，鼠王陛下。

新鼠王 ▸ 明天，你們每個人會帶著一支隊伍從秘密通道進入城堡裡，你們成功地進去之後，我向你們保證，所有在魔幻世界的豬都將免於被野狼攻擊的恐懼。

野狼 ▸ （大聲地抗議）那給我的「吃到飽」的保證呢？

新鼠王 ▸ （對野狼眨了一下眼）那個嘛，我只保證所有在魔幻世界的豬會安全不受野狼攻擊，一旦我征服了小男孩的那個世界，你可以吃所有的煙燻豬，也就是培根，吃到你心滿意足為止，聽起來如何呢？

野狼 ▸ 聽起來很可口！

三隻小豬 ▸ （試著岔開這不舒服的話題）萬一時尚王的侍衛就在通道等著突襲我們，怎麼辦？

新鼠王 ▸ 記得，不要奮戰到最後一口氣！立刻投降，讓他們覺得自己安全了！

野狼 ▸ （賊笑）我們會等到他們覺得自己已經沒有立即危險，然後在他們沒有預料的狀況下出擊！

新鼠王 ▸ 現在何不都去穿上我們的服裝呢？我們可是有一個化裝舞會要參加呢！

野狼 ▸ 當然好！

Phrases & Sentence Patterns 慣用語 & 句型

❶ keep someone off balance 使感到驚訝的；毫無防備的

❷ make a fool of oneself 出糗

❸ You've got my word. 我保證

❹ have freedom from 免於⋯

❺ a.k.a. 為 as known as 的縮寫，意思是「又名」「亦稱」

❻ what if 如果⋯（尤指糟糕的情況出現）⋯怎麼辦？

❼ out of danger 脫離險境

❽ Shall we ⋯?（提議時）我們做⋯好嗎？

  Cultural Note

In the old days, Halloween was more about costume parties and games. Old candies included candy corn, caramel apples, popcorn balls, and other handmade treats. However, in the 70s, rumor had it that people were putting razor blades in apples and poison in the popcorn balls. Ever since, non factory-sealed treats have been considered unsafe for children. Nowadays, when kids go trick-or-treating door to door, they might receive candy corn, tootsie rolls, suckers, and various min candy bars. Another feature of the Halloween season is pumpkins. There are pumpkin fields where parents like to take their children to pick out their own

pumpkins. People like to put a couple of pumpkins in the front yard, usually by the front door to add some seasonal decoration. Carving jack-o-lanterns out of pumpkins is also popular. It's common to find pumpkin carving patterns in stores. Therefore, if you feel that you're not artistic, you'll be able to carve a good pumpkin using a pattern that'll impress the trick-or-treaters at your door!

文化角落

　　過去的萬聖節主要是以裝扮派對和遊戲為主，那時的糖果包括玉米糖果（註）、焦糖蘋果、爆米花球和其他手工糖果。不過到了 70 年代，有謠言說有人將刀片放到蘋果裡，在爆米花球裡下毒。從此之後，非工廠生產包裝好的糖果，都被認為可能對小孩子產生危險。如今，當小孩挨家挨戶討萬聖節糖果時，他們可能會收到玉米糖果、*tootsie roll* 軟糖、棒棒糖，和各式各樣迷你糖果棒。萬聖節季節的另一個特色是南瓜。父母喜歡帶著小孩去南瓜園挑選自己的南瓜，人們也喜歡在住家前院，擺上兩顆應景南瓜，通常會放在靠前門的地方。刻南瓜也很受歡迎，而且很容易在店家找到刻南瓜的圖案。所以，即便你覺得自己沒什麼藝術天份，也是可以利用圖案刻出一顆好看的萬聖節南瓜，讓來討糖果吃的人對你的成品讚賞一番！

　　註：*candy corn* 長得像玉米筍，會依不同節日製成不同造型，萬聖節是 *candy corn* 會做成一顆南瓜。

Act Eight Scene 2

 ★ ★ 🎧 MP3 37

At the Masquerade Ball, the guests are excited about posing for photographs and tagging themselves on the Facebook page Tim set up called "Sparkling Splendid Summer Blast." ★ ★

Prince Charming — *(approaching Snow White from across the room)* I love your costume! It really brings out your beautiful dark hair and rosy cheeks.

Snow White — Thank you! Your white horse mask is very eye-catching too.

Prince Charming — Oh, my costume is not nearly as lovely as yours. My costume is inspired by my favorite white horse! How did you come up with yours?

Snow White — I was inspired by a movie called 'Catwoman'. My friend Tim showed me how to watch it on Amazon Prime Instant Video.

Prince Charming — Catwoman? Movie? Amazon? Those words are all so exotic to me. You're a very intelligent woman. Tonight is my lucky night!

Snow White (*blushing*) Thank you for the compliment.

Prince Charming Would you give me the pleasure of this dance?

Prince Charming and Snow White hold hands and join the rest of the guests on the dance floor. Outside the castle, the Three Little Pigs and their teams start entering the tunnels. Soon, the smell of grilled sweet corn sidetracks them and they quickly become sitting ducks for the King's Knights. They are all quickly captured and locked up in the dungeon. The Three Little Pigs, regarded as being kidnapped by the new Mouse King, are quickly released and they're invited to join the party.

King Stylish (*announcing the good news*) These Three Little Pigs had been kidnapped by the new Mouse King to help his mice invade the castle through our secret tunnels. My Knights were able to liberate them!

The Three Little Pigs wave to the guests.

King Stylish (*proudly*) And because of our thorough planning and watertight defense, we were able to thwart the attack!

The ballroom guests erupt in a thunderous cheer!

King Stylish — To celebrate our victory, please enjoy the catering provided by the Witch of the Candy House before the next dance!

在化裝舞會上，賓客們非常興奮地擺姿勢拍照，同時在提姆開的臉書專頁「繽紛絢麗之夏日狂歡」上標註自己。

白馬王子 —（從舞廳另一邊往白雪公主走過去）我喜歡妳的服裝，非常能襯托出妳美麗的烏黑秀髮與玫瑰紅雙頰。

白雪公主 — 謝謝！你白馬的面具也很引人注意。

白馬王子 — 喔，我的服裝完全比不上妳那可愛的服裝，我服裝的靈感是來自我最愛的白馬！妳的靈感來自哪裡呢？

白雪公主 — 是一部叫「貓女」的電影給我的靈感，我的朋友提姆跟我說過如何從亞馬遜線上即時電影頻道看電影。

白馬王子 — 貓女？電影？亞馬遜？這些字聽起來都非常具有異國風味，妳真是一個非常聰明的女人，今晚真是我的幸運之夜！

白雪公主 —（臉紅）謝謝你的讚美。

白馬王子 — 我有這榮幸請妳跳這支舞嗎？

白馬王子和白雪公主手牽手，加入其他賓客的行列在舞池跳舞，在城堡外，三隻小豬和他們的隊友正要進入通道。不久，烤甜玉米的香味轉移了他們的注意力，很快地，他們就變成國王騎士輕而易舉可以擊敗的對手，挪到這裡一下就被抓走，並關在地窖裡了。因為三隻小豬被認為是遭新鼠王綁架，所以很快地就被釋放，並且受邀參加派對。

時尚王 （宣布好消息）這三隻小豬之前被鼠王綁架，協助他的鼠兵從秘密通道進來入侵城堡，我的騎士讓他們重獲自由！
三隻小豬向賓客揮手。

時尚王 （感到很自豪）此外，由於我們縝密的計畫和滴水不漏的防守，才能夠阻止攻擊！
舞廳上的賓客爆出雷聲般響亮的歡呼聲！

時尚王 為了慶祝我們的勝利，在進入下一支舞之前，請先享用由糖果屋巫婆所準備的美食美酒！

Phrases & Sentence Patterns慣用語 & 句型

❶ bring out 襯托出，凸顯，使更出色

❷ eye-catching 搶眼的；吸引人目光的

❸ Will you give me the pleasure of... ?（邀約時客氣禮貌地詢問）
我有這榮幸…？

❹ Sitting ducks：容易被攻擊或擊中的人事物（註：想像鴨子在水上游泳時很難捕抓，但若坐在一個定點時就非常好捕抓）

❺ lock up 關起來；鎖起來

❻ be regarded as 被視為

❼ watertight defense：滴水不漏的防守

❽ in a thunderous cheer 如雷般響亮的歡呼聲

Cultural Note

I once hosted a small potluck party, where people bring a dish to share with everybody else, and found three bowls of guacamole dip sitting on the table, each brought by a different guest! This situation is not that surprising because guacamole, a thick, avocado-based dip typically served with tortilla chips, is one of the most common appetizers at a party. There are a variety of recipes for making this dish. However, the basic ingredients include A LOT OF mashed avocados, chopped tomato, onion, cilantro, lime, and chilies. The way to eat it is very casual. You simply grab a tortilla chip and dip it into the guacamole (hence why it's called a "dip"). You can also grab several tortilla chips and scoop up some guacamole dip onto your plate and save yourself some trips to the table. In fact, as a common fruit in the American cultures, avocado is used in different dishes. Besides guacamole, avocado is used on sandwiches, mixed in salads, and in sushi! The California Roll, made with cucumber, imitation crabmeat, cream cheese, and avocado, is one of the most popular types of sushi in the U.S.

文化角落

筆者曾經舉辦一個小型自助式派對（*potluck party*），每個人帶一份菜餚來和其他人分享，不過意外發現桌上出現三碗酪梨醬（*guacamole dip*），每一碗都是不同的客人帶來的！這情況並不意外，因為酪梨醬這個以口感濃郁的酪梨為主的沾醬，是派對上很常見的開胃菜，一般都是搭配玉米洋芋片一起吃。做這個沾醬的食譜有很多版本，不過基本材料就是很多壓碎的酪梨、切丁番茄、洋蔥、香菜、萊姆和墨西哥辣椒醬。吃法很隨性，你可以拿片玉米洋芋片沾一口酪梨醬（所以才叫做「沾醬」）。你也可以一口氣拿很多片在自己的餐盤上，然後挖一大匙酪梨醬在旁邊，這樣就可以省下好幾趟來回餐桌拿沾醬。實際上，酪梨在美國飲食文化中是很普遍的水果，被用在許多的菜餚裡。除了酪梨醬之外，酪梨也被拿來放在三明治、沙拉和壽司裡！加州捲，在美國很受歡迎的其中一種壽司，主要材料就是小黃瓜、蟹肉、奶油起司和酪梨。

 **MP3 38**

While the guests are having fun at the party, Tim is monitoring the ballroom from the neighboring room using the baby monitor.

Tim (*talking to himself*) Something seems fishy. Where are the new Mouse King and the Wolf? (*He speaks to the Giant via the Walkie-Talkie.*) Can you put down that plate of food and search for the new Mouse King and the Wolf?

Giant Stop being so bossy! I was just about to have my first bite of the cake!

Tim NOW!

Giant (*putting down the plate*) Yes, sir!

Not long later, Tim notices something happening to the guests through the baby monitor. THEY ARE ALL SHRINKING TO THE SIZE OF HIS THUMB!

Giant (*elated when reporting to Tim*) Holy cow! Did you just see that?

Everyone is super petite now! I feel like a giant again!

Tim ► Get serious! Can you identify the new Mouse King and the Wolf from those who didn't get shrunk?

Giant ► Found them! Oh, no... they are throwing a net to capture all the guests and King Stylish!

Tim ► Run to me NOW!

While the Giant is running back to Tim, he comes across Puss in Boots in the hallway.

Puss in Boots ► Speaking of the devil.

Giant ► (*looking around*) Where is he? Wait, my wife always tells me to read between the lines and not always accept the literal meaning of an expression! So... I think 'the devil' refers to... me?

Puss in Boots ► Finally, you have shown some intelligence in your little brain. The Wizard sent his Golden

Bird to me and asked me to bring you this. (*He hands a bag to the Giant*.) I can't believe I'm running an errand for you!

Giant (*looking into the bag*) Great. All the ingredients I need to make the King's Pancakes! (*He hugs Puss in Boots*.) Thank you!

Puss in Boots (*pushing him away*) No public displays of affection, PLEASE! Oh, just an FYI... the kitchen is currently overrun by mice.

Giant Well, I don't know the recipe anyway. I gotta run! Later!

Puss in Boots (*smirking*) Alright! I'll just return to the kitchen and have some fun with the mice!

第三場

當賓客在派對上享樂時，提姆正在鄰近的房間透過嬰兒監視器監看舞廳。

提姆 （自言自語）怪怪的，鼠王和野狼跑去哪裡了？（透過對講機和巨人說話）你可以放下那盤食物，先找一下鼠王和

野狼嗎？

巨人　別這麼會指使人！我才剛要吃第一口蛋糕！

提姆　現在立刻找！

巨人　（放下盤子）遵命！
不久之後，提姆透過嬰兒監視器注意到賓客有了些變化，他們全都縮到僅有他的拇指一樣的大小了！

巨人　（興高采烈地跟提姆報告）我的天啊！你有看到嗎？每個人現在都變得超迷你的，我感覺又變回巨人了！

提姆　正經一點！你有辦法從沒被縮小的賓客當中找出鼠王和野狼嗎？

巨人　找到了！喔，不妙…他們正對著所有賓客和國王撒網。

提姆　立刻跑到我這裡來！
當巨人往提姆那邊跑過去時，他在走道撞見穿靴子的貓。

穿靴子的貓　真是説曹操，曹操就到。

巨人　（環顧了一下四周）他在哪裡！？等等，我老婆總是對我説，不要只聽字面上的意義，要讀出言外之意！所以…我想那「曹操」是…我？

穿靴子的貓　終於啊，你的小腦袋瓜裡面還有一點智商，巫師派他的金色小鳥來找我，要我將這個給你。（他將一袋東西遞給巨人）真不敢相信我竟然在為你跑腿！

| 巨人 | （往袋子裡瞧了一下）太棒了，所有我需要做國王鬆餅的材料都到齊！（他擁抱穿靴子的貓）謝謝你！ |

| 穿靴子的貓 | （將他推開）拜託，別在公眾場合耍肉麻！喔，順便告訴你⋯廚房目前鼠輩橫行。 |

| 巨人 | 那麼，反正我也不知道食譜，我得走了！再聊！ |

| 穿靴子的貓 | （促狹地笑著）好極了！讓我回去廚房和老鼠們玩一玩。 |

Phrases & Sentence Patterns慣用語 & 句型

❶ petite（嬌）小的，這字源自法文，petite 也常使用在買衣服的尺碼上面，除了有正常尺碼和大尺碼（plus-size）之外，也有小號（petite-size）尺碼給身材嬌小的人

❷ come across 巧遇

❸ speaking of the devil 說曹操，曹操就到

❹ read between the lines 讀出言外之意

❺ refer to 指得是⋯；意指⋯

❻ run an errand 跑腿

❼ public display of affection（尤指情侶）在公眾場合經由肢體接觸表達情感，例如牽手，接吻等

❽ FYI = for your information（用於提供某人你認為他可能需要知道的資訊時）供參考

The Puss in Boots character in the Brothers Grimm's fairy tale is a clever cat, who helps an ordinary young man to win a kingdom. The cat visits the king and brings him different things every day. He claims that all the gifts are from his lord, the Count, who is actually only a miller's son. One day, Puss in Boots arranged for his lord to meet the king and the princess. Then, he ventures his lives to trick a wizard into turning himself into a mouse. He catches the mouse and eats it, so the wizard's castle becomes his lord's place to entertain the king and the princess. Eventually, his lord becomes the king and Puss in Boots is his prime minster. In addition, The Cat in the Hat, a series of children books by Dr. Seuss, is another resourceful cat character with a lot of tricks to entertain children. Perhaps, besides the typical image of being independent, cats are also commonly seen as witty and resourceful animals across cultures.

文化角落

　　格林童話《穿靴子的貓》裡的主角是一隻聰明的貓，他幫助一個平凡的年輕人贏得一個王國。這隻貓每天拜訪國王並帶給他不同的東西，他宣稱這些東西都是他的主人，伯爵大人，請他帶過來的，但實際上這伯爵大人只是磨坊主人的兒子。有一天，穿靴子的貓安排他的主人和國王與公主見面，他先是冒著自己的生命危險，靠計謀讓一個巫師將自己變成一隻老鼠，他抓了老鼠並吃掉牠，巫師的城堡因此變成他主人的宮殿，可以用來招待國王和公主。最後，他的主人順利成為國王，穿靴子的貓變成首相。此外，《戴帽子的貓》這一系列童書（作者蘇斯博士 Dr. Seuss），裡面的貓也會變出很多把戲娛樂小孩。或許，貓除了給人一種很獨立的刻板形象之外，在不同文化中，帶給人的面貌也常常是隻有智慧且很有辦法的動物。

After passing by numerous rooms full of mice, the Giant finally locates Tim in the Mirror Room.

Tim — Great... you made it! We must get to the Wizard's house to find some tools we can use to save everyone!

Giant — How're we gonna get there?

Tim — Shhh... quiet. Someone's coming. I think I smell a rat! Quick! Get under this invisibility cape!

Tim and the Giant huddle under the protection of the cape.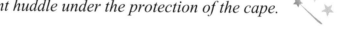

Giant — *(whispering)* Great idea, we're outnumbered. It wouldn't be fun to expose our whereabouts. By the way, I got all the ingredients to make the King's Pancakes! But it's crowded in the kitchen with a full house of mice!

Tim — Yeah, too many cooks in the kitchen is never a good thing.

Giant ▸ I'm anxious! When can I cook my pancakes?

Tim ▸ We'll try to find something at the Wizard's home to cook your pancakes.

Giant ▸ We also need to get the recipe.

Tim ▸ Yes, I know. (*He looks around.*) I think it's safe at the moment. I'll turn on the GPS and we can use the *'Essence of Rainbow'* magic powder to hightail it out of here.

Soon after Tim sprinkles the 'Essence of Rainbow' magic powder, a desk in the Mirror Room moves toward them and a drawer opens. Tim looks into the drawer and sees a small colorful whirlpool spinning inside. He grabs the Giant by his left hand and slowly reaches his right hand into the whirlpool. They both are sucked into the whirlpool and eventually land inside the Wizard's home.

Tim ▸ Gee whiz, there must be a better way to travel within this world. I feel dizzy now.

Giant ▸ Me too.

Tim ▸ My GPS shows the secret chamber over there.

Tim swipes the door's sensor pad with the Wizard's digital key. As they enter the chamber, they can't take their eyes off the shelves loaded with various technological gadgets.

Tim Wow, the Wizard sure is a big collector of high-tech gadgets! (*He hands a digital pocket scale to the Giant.*) Grab anything else you think might be useful.

Giant I'm on it!

Tim Here, take this electronic toothbrush too. Your breath really stinks!

Giant Hey, being your sidekick doesn't give you the right to be so brutally honest!

Tim Sorry dude! But I really can't put up with it anymore.

 第四場

在經過無數間充滿老鼠的房間之後，巨人終於找到位於鏡廳的提姆了。

提姆　太棒了…你順利找到這裡！我們必須趕去巫師家去找有用的工具來拯救大家！

巨人　我們要怎麼過去？

提姆　噓…安靜，有人來了，我嗅到鼠味（暗喻事情有可疑之處）！快！躲到這隱形斗篷底下。
提姆和巨人蜷縮在斗篷的保護之下。

巨人　（小小聲地說）真是太棒的主意了，現在我們人數上完全暫居下風，暴露我們的蹤跡真的不太妙，對了，我拿到做國王鬆餅的所有材料了！可是廚房現在滿屋鼠輩，可擠得哩。

提姆　是啊，廚房人多手雜，難辦事。

巨人　好焦慮！我什麼時候才可以做我的鬆餅！？

提姆　我們可以在巫師家找可以煮你的鬆餅的器具。

巨人　我們也還得拿到食譜。

提姆　是的，我知道。（他環顧四週）我想暫時安全了，我來打開衛星導航，然後用彩虹元素魔法粉末迅速離開這裡。

　　當提姆灑了一些彩虹元素的魔法粉末。不久之後，鏡廳裡的一個書桌往他們這方向移動過來，一個抽屜在他們面前打開。提姆往抽屜裡一探，看到一個小小的七彩漩渦正在快速轉動著。他左手抓著巨人，右手慢慢地伸向那漩渦。很快地，他們兩個都被捲進去，最後在巫

281

師的屋內著地。

提姆 ► 我的老天爺啊，一定有比較好的方式在這個世界移動，我頭都暈了。

巨人 ► 我也是。

提姆 ► 我的衛星導航顯示密室在那邊。
提姆用巫師的數位鑰匙刷了一下感應板，當他們進到密室時，目光完全離不開放滿各式高科技用品的架子。

提姆 ► 哇，巫師真的是高科技玩意的大收藏家耶！（他遞給巨人一個數位可攜帶式磅秤）拿任何你覺得可能可以用到的東西吧。

巨人 ► 恩，我正在進行！

提姆 ► 這電動牙刷也拿著吧，你有很重的口臭！

巨人 ► 嘿，只因為我是你的副手不代表你有權利可以這麼毫無顧忌地說實話！

提姆 ► 老兄，真不好意思！但我實在無法再忍受了。

Phrases & Sentence Patterns 慣用語 & 句型

❶ smell a rat 發覺有可疑之處，感到其中有詐
❷ too many cooks，取自 too many cooks spoil the soup，指得是，人多反而誤事

❸ under the protection of…在…的保護之下

❹ hightail it out of here 迅速離開某處，hightail 的意思即是迅速逃離；匆忙離開

❺ cannot take one's eyes off... 目光完全離不開…

❻ I'm on it. 正要進行；正要處理

❼ brutally honest 毫無顧忌的説實話（不去考慮會不會傷害到對方的感受）

❽ put up with 忍受

Cultural Note

    In the previous culture note, we talked about the positive images of cats in stories. On the other hand, black cats are generally seen as a symbol of evil omens in U.S. culture. For example, people believe that a black cat crossing your path will bring you very back luck. Black cats are commonly paired with witches because they're believed to be able to sense the presence of spirits. In western culture, witches were generally regarded as evil, especially during the witch-hunting period in the 17th century. In fact, whether cats are seen as good or evil really depends on the culture. For the Ancient Egyptians, cats were sacred animals to the cat goddess Bastet and treated as royalty. Mummified cats have been found all over her temples. When you have a chance to visit the Metropolitan Museum of New York, be sure to visit the galleries of Egyptian Art. You will see collections of cat statues or mummies of cats from Ancient Egyptian.

文化角落

　　前面的文化角落我們提到貓在不同故事中所呈現的正面形象。另一方面來說，人們相信黑貓經過你要走的路會帶來不幸。由於黑貓被認為可以感受到靈魂的存在，他們很常與女巫被湊成一對。在西方文化裡，女巫一般被認為是邪惡的，尤其在 17 世紀獵女巫的那段時期。實際上，貓究竟被視為善或惡因不同文化而有所不同。古埃及人視貓為女神 Bastet 身邊的神聖動物，受到皇族般尊貴的對待，在女神廟四周曾找到許多木乃伊貓。有機會造訪紐約的大都會博物館時，一定要參觀一下埃及館，在那裡你可以看到許多貓雕像或是從古埃及找到的貓木乃伊。

Scene 5 MP3 40

Tim (*continuing to put gadgets into his backpack*) Hmm... remote control helicopters are fun. Oh, this lithium-ion cordless chainsaw and electric skateboard might really come in handy!

By the time Tim and the Giant return to the Mirror Room, they check the situation in the ballroom from the baby monitor immediately. All the guests have the look of doom and gloom. As Tim and the Giant listen to the new Mouse King's conversation with people in the ballroom, they are busy preparing to break in and save everyone.

New Mouse King (*laughing widely*) Five years ago, my father was murdered by the Wizard's Nutcracker. Now you all should prepare to die!

King Stylish You know the Wizard didn't mean to hurt your father.

New Mouse King (*replying bitterly*) But he did, didn't he. And look where he is now? What a coward!

Dairy Queen My dear friend, you know the truth. He exiled himself to another world to repent what he did.

King Stylish — We would sincerely like to make up for your loss in every way possible. Hopefully, we can learn to get along with one another.

Dairy Queen — Say, your mice have always loved our Gouda and Provolone cheese! We could bring you on board as our business partner!

New Mouse King — No thanks. Once I rule the World of Wonderland, my mice can have all the cheese they want.

King Stylish — Please think twice before you say no! Don't do anything on impulse that you will definitely regret later.

New Mouse King — (*shaking his head*) NEVER!

While the new Mouse King is busy preparing a spell to turn all the guests into cheese statues, two remote control helicopters fly into the ballroom and begin showering shredded cheese all around the room. All the mice, including the new Mouse King, couldn't help but look up with their mouths wide open trying to catch the cheese.

第五場

提姆　（繼續將小東西放到他的背包裡）恩…遙控直升機很好玩，喔，這鋰電池免插頭電鋸和電動滑板也許會有用！
提姆和巨人回到鏡廳之後，立刻從嬰兒監視器查看舞廳的情況。所有的賓客看起來都一臉憂鬱無望的表情。當提姆和巨人聽著新鼠王和其他人在舞廳的對話時，也同時準備著闖入舞廳救大家的東西。

新鼠王　（狂笑）五年前，我父王被巫師的胡桃鉗謀殺了。現在你們等著陪葬吧！

時尚王　你知道巫師並不是故意傷害你父親的。

新鼠王　（語帶憤怒的回答）可是他就是殺害了我父王，不是嗎？你們看，他現在人在哪了呢？真是懦弱的傢伙！

冰雪皇后　我親愛的朋友，你是知道真相的，他是將自己流放到人類世界去懺悔自己的過錯。

時尚王　我們誠心地希望以各種方式補償你失去你的父親這件事，也希望可以彼此學著和平相處。

冰雪皇后　就是啊，你的鼠民們一向喜歡我家的高達起司和普羅旺斯起司！我們可以讓你加入，一起合夥做生意！

新鼠王　不用了，等我統治了魔幻世界之後，我的鼠民們就可以有吃不完的起司。

時尚王　在你拒絕我們之前請再三思一下！別在衝動之下做任何你之後絕對會後悔的事。

新鼠王　（搖搖頭）我絕不會後悔的！
當新鼠王忙著準備咒語，要將所有的賓客變成起司雕像時，兩台遙控直升機飛進舞廳，開始滿屋子撒下起司條。所有的老鼠，包括新鼠王，都忍不住抬頭，並張開嘴巴試著接住落下的起司。

Phrases & Sentence Patterns 慣用語 & 句型

❶ come in handy 有用；派上用場
❷ doom and gloom 感到毫無希望
❸ （not）mean to （非）故意
❹ make up for 彌補；補償
❺ in every way 在各方面
❻ get along with 與…相處融洽
❼ on impulse 一時衝動
❽ cannot help but + 原型動詞 忍不住…；禁不住…

Cultural Note

You might already notice the expression "What's up?" appearing several times in the story. In fact, the expression "What's up?" is a very common greeting in the U.S. However, during my first year staying in the U.S., I was very confused by this

expression. For example, an American friend I saw in the hallway looked at me and said, "What's up?" as she walked by. I wondered why my friend did not stop and at least have a short conversation with me. Later, I realized that this expression simply means "Hello." Therefore, unless you really have something to say, people usually will just give you a smile and continue on their way. In the story, what makes it funny is an unexpected long explanation of how the character feels when the other askes him/her "What's up?" The reason is that in reality, a very common response is "not too much."

文化角落

　　你應該注意到 What's up? 在本故事中經出現了好幾次。實際上，What's up?這句話在美國是很常聽到的問候語。不過，筆者在美國生活的第一年，曾因這問候語而感到困惑。舉例來說，一個美國朋友在走廊看到筆者時，說了一句 "What's up?" 然後就擦身而過。筆者當時在想，為什麼朋友沒有停下腳步，至少來個幾句簡短對話。後來才知道，原來這句話就只是在說「哈囉」。所以，除非你真的有什麼話要說，一般人通常都是回你一個微笑然後繼續趕他們的路。在本故事裡，好笑的點即是，當被問到 "What's up?" 時，角色卻丟了一個不預期且又臭又長的解釋，跟對方說他的感受。在現實生活中，很常見的回答是「老樣子」。

Three hours before the helicopters entered the ballroom, Tim and the Wizard had a conversation using their app to exchange information.

Wizard The Witch of the Candy House has been imprisoned in her basement.

Tim Oh no... is she okay?

Wizard She's fine. The Wolf, disguised as Little Red Riding Hood, tricked her into letting him enter her house. He then locked her up and found her Dwarf Cookie recipe!

Tim So that was how they were able to shrink the guests at the Masquerade Ball!

Wizard Yes. Puss in Boots is already en route to rescue her. You should meet up with them outside the castle.

Tim I don't know how to reach them. Maybe I can drop a pin in my Google Maps and share it with you?

Act Eight Scene 6

Wizard Perfect! I will contact Puss in Boots to let him know where to find you.

Tim Okay thanks. I'll keep you posted!

Tim, the Giant, the Witch, and Puss in Boots reunite at a location two miles away from the castle.

Tim I'm relieved to see you were found safe and sound! Great job Puss in Boots!

Puss in Boots (*taking his hat off and bowing proudly*) My pleasure.

Witch (*taking out a cookie from her bag*) Wanna try a cookie this time, my dearie?

Tim Uh... maybe later.

Witch You really ARE as stubborn as a mule!

Giant (*giving the Witch a big hug*) I'm sooooo happy to see you again. If you don't mind, can I have that cookie?

291

The Witch reluctantly gives the Giant the cookie.

Witch Oh, before I left my place, I cut the cheese...

Giant (*pinching his nose*) Ewww... stinky!

Witch What I meant is that I prepared a big bag of shredded cheese for the mice.

Tim Then we can use what they love against them!

Witch You read my mind!

Tim Hey, I've got an idea! But I'll need help from somebody from on the inside.

Tim quickly texts Cinderella.

Tim The Giant has all the ingredients for making your King's Pancakes and the cookware to make them outdoors. We will need LOTS OF pancakes for all the guests. He can be your sous-chef.

Witch ▶ No problem. Making pancakes is a piece of cake!

Tim ▶ Here are the manuals for the electronic cookware, just in case.

Witch ▶ Thank you, my dearie!

第六場

在兩台遙控直升機飛進舞廳的三小時前，提姆和巫師透過他們的應用程式交換訊息。

巫師 ▶ 糖果屋的巫婆被囚禁在她的地下室。

提姆 ▶ 不會吧⋯她還好嗎？

巫師 ▶ 她很好，野狼假扮成小紅帽騙她開門讓他進屋子裡，之後野狼就將她鎖起來，還找到了小矮人餅乾的食譜！

提姆 ▶ 原來他們是這樣才有辦法將化裝舞會上的賓客都縮小了！

巫師 ▶ 是的，穿靴子的貓已經在去救她的路上了，你應該和他們在城堡外會合。

提姆 ▶ 我不知道怎麼聯絡上他們，或許我可以在我的谷歌（Google）地圖上標記地點，分享給你看？

| 巫師 | 好極了！我會和穿靴子的貓聯絡，讓他知道怎麼找到你。 |

| 提姆 | 好，謝啦！我會隨時跟你報告新進度！
提姆、巨人、巫婆和穿靴子的貓在離城堡兩英哩外的地方會合了。 |

| 提姆 | 看到妳毫髮無傷真是令人鬆一口氣！穿靴子的貓，幹得好啊！ |

| 穿靴子的貓 | （脫掉帽子，自豪地鞠躬）這沒什麼，不用客氣。 |

| 巫婆 | （從她的袋子拿出一塊餅乾）親愛的，這次想試一下餅乾嗎？ |

| 提姆 | 哦…或許晚一點吧。 |

| 巫婆 | 你怎麼像驢子一樣固執到不行！ |

| 巨人 | （給巫婆一個大擁抱）我真的很高興再次見到妳，如果妳不介意的話，我可以吃那塊餅乾嗎？
巫婆不情願地將餅乾給了巨人。 |

| 巫婆 | 喔，在我離開我家之前，我放了一個屁… |

| 巨人 | （捏著鼻子）哎唷…很臭耶！ |

| 巫婆 | 我是指，我準備了一大袋起司條要給老鼠吃。 |

| 提姆 | 那麼我們就用他們的最愛來對付他們！ |

巫婆	你懂我的心！

提姆	嘿，我有個主意，不過我需要找一個內應幫我忙。 提姆快速地傳簡訊給灰姑娘。

提姆	巨人有做國王鬆餅所需要的所有材料和在戶外煮東西的廚具，我們會需要很多鬆餅供給所有賓客吃，他可以當你的副廚。

巫婆	沒問題，做鬆餅是輕而易舉的事！

提姆	這裡是一些電子廚具操作手冊，以防萬一。

巫婆	親愛的，謝謝你唷！

Phrases & Sentence Patterns慣用語 & 句型

❶ en route: 在路上（= on the way）
❷ keep someone posted 隨時報告新進度
❸ my pleasure 這沒什麼，不用客氣
❹ safe and sound 毫髮無傷
❺ as stubborn as a mule 像驢子一樣固執到不行
❻ cut the cheese 放屁
❼ read someone's mind 看出（某人的）心思；猜出（某人）想什麼
❽ on the inside 在機構或組織內部而知道清況的人；參與內部機密的人

The animation Ratatouille (2007) is a movie about a rat, Remy, who has a passion for cooking. He also happens to have a highly developed sense of taste and smell. Remy meets a garbage boy, Linguini, who works at Gustav's restaurant and struggles to keep his job. The pair make an agreement to cooperate with each other so that Linguini can keep his job and Remy can fulfill his dream of becoming a chef. In the movie, French words, such as "Bon appetite" and "sous-chef" are often used. In fact, there are many French words and expressions used in American English, especially when it comes to food. For example, the French words "appetizers", "entrees", and "a la carte" dishes are all commonly used on menus in American restaurants. Finally, the "omelet" is a common breakfast/brunch food item, while a frozen "quiche" can be easily found in any supermarket. Of course, the pronunciation of these words typically has a touch of an American accent!

文化角落

　　動畫《料理鼠王》（Ratatouille, 2007）描述一隻熱愛料理的老鼠小米（Remy）的故事。除了熱愛料理，小米剛好也有高度靈敏的味覺與嗅覺。他認識了在古斯塔夫（Gustav）餐廳收垃圾的男孩小林（Linguine，其名和義大利一種麵條同名），他很努力要保住自己這份工作。他們於是達成一個協議，要一起合作讓小林保住他的工作，而小米可以實現自己當主廚的夢想。在電影中常可聽到法文，像是 Bon appetite（祝有好胃口）和 sous-chef（副廚）。事實上，在美式英文裡沿用了許多法文字和句子，尤其是和吃有關的部分。例如，appetizers（開胃菜）、entrees（主菜）和單點（a la carte）都是美國餐廳的菜單裡很常出現的法文字。最後，歐姆蛋（omelet）這個字是出現在早餐或早午餐選項上，而在任何超市都可以輕易地找到冷凍的法式鹹派（quiche）。當然，這些字的發音通常都帶著一點美國的口音！

Act Nine 🎧 MP3 42

Reconciliation

While the mice are busy catching the falling shredded cheese, Cinderella directs the band to play some heavy metal music. Small as they are now, the music is played loudly enough to cover the noise outside. Tim is using the lithium-ion powered chainsaw to break the ballroom door. After destroying the doorknob, Puss in Boots breaks through the door and rides into the ballroom on the electric skateboard.

Scene 1

Puss in Boots — *(throwing a lariat at the mice, capturing them one by one and putting them into his bag)* Yeehaw! The more, the merrier! Keep them coming!

Soon, all the mice had been captured and stuffed into his bag, except for the new Mouse King and the Wolf. In the meantime, Tim uses his chainsaw to cut open the net to release all the guests.

New Mouse King — *(realizing what happened and wailing)* Oh my... I thought I was eating cheese but instead all I get

is egg on my face! (*He kneels on the floor and starts to weep.*) Now I'm a dead duck.

The Wolf (*weeping*) I think you mean a DEAD MOUSE, Master.

New Mouse King (*cuddling with the Wolf and weeping in unison*) Stop it! You're crying like a baby.

The Wolf (*sniffling*) I'm sorry. Only bacon can make me feel better now.

New Mouse King I've failed you. I don't think you'll be having all the bacon in the human world now.

Upon hearing the bad news, the Wolf starts weeping even louder.

King Stylish My dear Mouse King, chill out! It's not as bad as you think.

New Mouse King But... I've failed to fulfill my father's expectations. All his life, he endeavored to ensure all mice are well liked. Something I think is mission impossible unless I can cast a spell on the humans to change how they feel about mice.

Tim ⟶ Your Mousety, let me boost your spirits. I'll show you a place where all animals are loved by humans, especially kids.

New Mouse King ⟶ *(his eyes wide open)* Is there such a place like that?

Tim hooks up his laptop to the mini-projector and displays a YouTube video on the wall. In the video, people are holding balloons and are being greeted by mascots.

第九幕

和解

　　當老鼠們忙著接掉下來的起司時，灰姑娘指揮樂團演奏一些重金屬搖滾樂，即便他們都被縮小了，所演奏的音樂還是大到足以掩蓋外面的噪音。提姆正在用鋰電池電鋸，要破門進入舞廳。門把被破壞之後，穿靴子的貓穿過門，踩在電動滑板上進入舞廳。

穿靴子的貓 ⟶ （用繩套套老鼠，將他們一一放進自己的袋子裡）嘿哈！抓越多越開心！繼續來啊！
　　很快地，除了新鼠王和野狼之外，所有的老鼠都被抓走，

並塞進他的袋子裡。同時間,提姆用他的電鋸切開網子,
釋放了所有的賓客。

新鼠王　（意識到發生了什麼事,開始嚎啕大哭）喔天啊…我以為
我只是吃個起司,但迎面而來的卻是羞辱!（他跪在地板
上並開始哭泣）現在我就像隻死鴨子,是個徹頭徹尾的失
敗者。

野狼　（哭著說）主人,我想你該說自己是隻死老鼠吧。

新鼠王　（和野狼抱在一起哭泣）別說了!你怎麼哭得跟一個小嬰
兒一樣。

野狼　（抽了一下鼻涕）真抱歉,現在只有培根可以讓我開心一
點。

新鼠王　我讓你失望了,我覺得你不會得到人類世界所有的培根
了。
一聽到這壞消息,野狼哭得更大聲。

時尚王　我親愛的鼠王,冷靜下來!情況沒有你想得這麼糟。

新鼠王　可是…我沒能夠完成我父王的期望,他終其一生都致力於
確保老鼠們能被喜愛,我覺得除非我對人類下咒語,改變
他們對老鼠的觀感,不然這根本是一件不可能達成的任
務。

提姆　鼠王陛下,讓我幫你提振精神吧,我給你看一個地方,在
那裡所有的動物都受到人類喜愛,尤其深受孩子們的喜
愛。

新鼠王 （睜大雙眼）有這樣一個地方嗎？

提姆將他的筆記型電腦接上迷你投影機，並在一面牆上播放 YouTube 影片。在影片裡，人們拿著汽球並且受到吉祥物的歡迎。

 ## Phrases & Sentence Patterns慣用語 & 句型

❶ The more, the merrier！越多越令人開心

❷ egg on your face 感到尷尬或被羞辱（通常是因為一件你做的或說的蠢事）

❸ dead duck（尤指因過錯或判斷失誤造成的）不太可能成功的人或不太可能持續下去計畫

❹ in unison 共同；一起

❺ fail someone 讓某人失望；辜負某人（的期望等）

❻ chill out 放輕鬆；冷靜（= relax, calm down）

❼ boost one's spirit 提振精神

❽ hook up（將電子設備）連接；聯播

 ## Cultural Note

As you have figured out by now, when someone "cuts the cheese" at the dinner table, it means that he/she just passed gas. Besides using cheese as a metaphor, beans are another food that is often related to the increased intestinal activity. There is even a children's song for it called "Beans, Beans,

the Musical Fruit." The song has various versions, but I've included one version for you!

> Beans, beans, the musical fruit,
> The more you eat, the more you toot!
> The more you toot, the better you feel,
> So let's eat beans with every meal!

Beans are very common dishes at the dinner table. One of the most common ways to make beans is a dish simply called baked beans. For some Americans, baked beans are seen as one of their staple comfort foods. However, although Americans love their beans, they usually find Chinese bean desserts, such as red bean soup, strange. They cannot fathom the idea of beans being used in a dessert, not to mention making them into a sweet soup!

你現在應該已經知道，當某人在晚餐上「切起司」（cut the cheese），意思是他放屁了。除了拿起司當比喻之外，豆子是另一個常拿來和活躍的腸胃蠕動聯想在一起的食物，甚至還有首兒歌「豆子，豆子，悅耳的豆子」。這首歌有很多不同版本，這裡是其中一個版本！

豆子，豆子，悅耳的水果，
吃得越多，屁放得越多！
屁放得越多，越舒服通暢，
就讓豆子伴我們每一餐！

豆子是晚餐餐桌上很常見的菜色之一，一個最常料理的方式是烤豆子，對很多美國人而言，烤豆子是一道撫慰人心的主食。不過，雖然美國人喜歡他們的豆子料理，他們常覺得中國的豆類點心非常奇怪，像是紅豆湯。他們沒辦法想像將豆子做成甜點，更不用說煮成甜湯！

Scene 2 🎧 MP3 43

The new Mouse King is fascinated with what he sees in the YouTube video and even smiles when he sees a long line of kids waiting to take their photos with those mascots.

New Mouse King — Unbelievable? Everyone is getting in line to hug that large smiley mouse! I like his outfit too! Where is this place?

Tim — It's called Disney World, in Orlando, Florida.

New Mouse King — Can you refer me to that mouse? I would like to consult with him and learn how to become popular.

Tim — Sure. His role is in high demand, especially during summer vacation. You can't miss him.

The Wolf — Well, I do LOOOOVE kids. It sounds like an interesting gig!

Tim — Go for it! As long as you promise not to hurt anyone. Then you can bring home a lot of

bacon too!

The Wolf → Yuuuummy!

Tim → Well, it is a HOT position. Maybe you'll find these two gadgets helpful!

Tim takes out a handheld fan and an electric shaver for the Wolf.

The Wolf → (*turning on the handheld fan and blowing the breeze towards his face*) This feels cool!

Tim → (*talking to the new Mouse King*) If you would consider forgiving the Wizard, I think he could arrange a trip to Orlando for the two of you.

New Mouse King → (*replying proudly*) Since I wish to meet my father's expectation, I'll agree to talk to him this time.

Tim gives the Wizard a video call immediately and describes what happened.

Tim → Here is the Mouse King on the phone for ya!

Act Nine　Scene 2

New Mouse King　(*getting the phone from Tim*) Hello Wizard.

Wizard　Hi, Your Mousety. Thank you for being willing to give me a clean slate.

New Mouse King　Not quite yet... not until you introduce me to that big-eared mouse.

Wizard　No problem. Would you like to take a road trip with me down to Orlando?

New Mouse King　That sounds great!

The Wolf　Hey, don't forget ME!

Wizard　Okay Wolf, you can join, too. Please come with Tim to Chicago.

第二場

　　新鼠王興奮又激動地看著 YouTube 的影片，甚至當他看到小孩子大排長龍，等著和吉祥物拍照時，自己也跟著微笑。

新鼠王 ▶ 真是令人難以置信！每個人都排隊要擁抱那隻笑咪咪的大老鼠！我也喜歡他的服裝！這是哪裡呢？

提姆 ▶ 這地方叫做迪士尼世界，在佛羅里達的奧蘭多（Orlando）。

新鼠王 ▶ 你可以介紹那隻老鼠給我認識嗎？我想要跟他諮詢，向他學習如何變得受歡迎。

提姆 ▶ 好啊，他的角色需求很高，尤其是在暑假期間，你絕對可以碰到他的。

野狼 ▶ 那個，我超愛小孩的，聽起來會是很有趣的工作！

提姆 ▶ 去爭取吧！只要你答應不傷害任何人。這樣你也可以賺到錢帶著培根回家！

野狼 ▶ 好吃耶！

提姆 ▶ 喔，這是一個受歡迎又非常悶熱的職缺，或許這些小東西對你有幫助！
提姆拿出手持電風扇和電動刮鬍刀並交給野狼。

野狼 ▶ （打開手持電風扇，微風就朝著他的臉上吹）感覺很涼爽耶！

提姆 ▶ （對新鼠王說）如果你願意考慮原諒巫師，我想他可以為你們兩人安排去奧蘭多的旅行。

新鼠王 ▶ （擺出驕傲的神情回答）既然我希望完成我父王的期望，

我同意就這次和他通一下話。
提姆立刻打視訊電話給巫師，跟他描述發生了什麼事。

提姆 ▶ 新鼠王就在電話這頭等你！

新鼠王 ▶ （從提姆那接過電話）哈囉巫師。

巫師 ▶ 嗨，鼠王陛下，謝謝你願意與我盡棄前嫌，重新開始。

新鼠王 ▶ 還沒完全釋懷…要等你介紹那隻大耳朵老鼠給我認識再說。

巫師 ▶ 沒問題，你想不想和我一起開車旅行到奧蘭多？

新鼠王 ▶ 聽起來很不錯！

野狼 ▶ 嘿，別忘了我！

巫師 ▶ 好，野狼，你也加入我們，請都跟提姆到芝加哥吧。

Phrases & Sentence Patterns 慣用語 & 句型

❶ get in line 排隊
❷ refer someone to 介紹某人給…認識
❸ in high demand 需求量很高
❹ Go for it. 去做吧；去爭取吧
❺ bring home the bacon 掙錢
❻ a hot position 在此一語雙關，指得是「受歡迎的職位」也同時是「很熱的職位」因為要穿上動物玩偶的服裝

❼ meet one's expectation 符合某人的期望
❽ a clean slate 盡棄前嫌，重新開始

Cultural Note

Route 66 was one of the original highways in the U.S. Highway System. It originally ran from Chicago, Illinois, all the way to Santa Monica, California, which significantly helped those who traveled to the West Coast of the U.S. When Route 66 was prosperous, it supported the economies of the small towns through which the road passed. Route 66 was later replaced by the Interstate Highway System, which bypassed these small towns and promoted quicker travel. In the animated movie Cars, you can see the rise and fall of a small town situated on Route 66 after the interstate is built. Nowadays, the extensive Interstate Highway System makes it very convenient to plan a road trip to go anywhere within the United States. As there are nine climate zones in the Continental United States National Centers for Environmental Information, one of the best aspects about taking a road trip is being able to appreciate the changing composition of the vegetation along the way and observing the geographical changes.

文化角落

　　第 66 公路是美國高速公路系統最初的其中一條公路。最初的路線是從伊利諾利州（*Illinois*）的芝加哥，一路直通加州的聖摩尼卡（*Santa Monica*），這條公路大大地幫助了那些需要前往美國西岸的旅人。當第 66 號公路還很繁榮的時候，也帶動沿途所經過的小鎮的經濟。後來公路被跨州高速公路系統取代，為了提高行進速度，不再經過這些小鎮。在《汽車總動員》（*Cars*）這部動畫裡，就可以看到第 66 號公路會經過的某小鎮，因為跨州公路興建好的興衰。現在，擴建後的跨州高速公路系統，讓安排一趟美國境內的公路旅行變得很方便。因為美國本土一共跨九個氣候區（國家環境資訊中心 *National Centers for Environmental Information*），公路之旅的好處之一是可以欣賞沿途不同的自然景觀，並觀察地理變化。

Cinderella's Stepmother: (glaring at the new Mouse King) Okay! After your happy conclusion with the Wizard, can you now change us back to our normal size? This is driving me nuts!

The new Mouse King shows a look of remorse.

Tim   Looks like that is out of his hands. Sometimes magic is like tipping. Once given, you can't just take it back.

Suddenly, the door from the kitchen swings open. The Giant is pushing a tower of King's Pancakes into the ballroom. Seeing the pancakes is really a sight for sore eyes for all the guests, who've worked up a tremendous appetite. Everyone cheers! After the guests have their fill of the King's Pancakes, they all return to their normal size.

Cinderella's Stepmother   I was bummed out earlier, but I feel ecstatic now!

Tim   Hahaha. My grandma always tells me that good things come in small packages. But apparently that doesn't apply to you.

Cinderella's Stepmother — Nope! Being small makes me anxious.

Tim — I can see that.

The Giant, now back to his enormous size, walks proudly up to Tim and gives him a GIANT hug!

Tim — (*looking up to speak to the Giant*) You are a true giant again!

Giant — (*gleefully*) Yes I am! Now you'll have to watch out whenever you get a rise out of me!

Tim — No kidding! I am so happy for you! You can finally climb up your beanstalk and go home!

Giant — Thanks. I do miss my wife.

Tim — (*nudging the Giant*) Absence makes the heart grow fonder, doesn't it big guy?

King Stylish — Tonight is a night worth celebrating! (*He raises his glass to propose a toast.*) To Tim and his bravery!

Everyone ► To Tim and his bravery!

Tim ► Thank you. Oh, we should take a happy ending group photo together. (*He takes out his selfie stick and asks everyone to gather together around him.*) I will notify you all once the photos are posted on Instagram.

King Stylish ► Tim, after you arrive home, please send my regards to the Wizard and let him know that he's welcome home anytime.

Tim ► Will do.

灰姑娘的繼母 ► （憤怒地看著新鼠王）可好啦！你和巫師有了快樂的結局之後，可以將我們都變回正常的尺寸嗎？這樣子讓我快抓狂了！
新鼠王一副懊悔自責的表情。

提姆 ► 看來他也束手無策，有些魔法就像給小費一樣，一旦付出去了，就沒辦法再收回來。
忽然間，廚房的門打開了，巨人推著國王鬆餅的高塔進入舞廳。所有賓客都非常高興看到鬆餅，瞬間都胃口大開。每個人都歡呼著！賓客吃了國王鬆餅之後，都恢復到原本的尺寸。

灰姑娘的繼母 ▸ 我之前還覺得很憂鬱，現在真的芳心大悅！

提姆 ▸ 哈哈哈，我奶奶總是跟我說，好的東西不見得都很大，可是顯然這道理不適用在你身上。

灰姑娘的繼母 ▸ 完全無法適用。小尺寸讓我感到焦慮。

提姆 ▸ 完全看得出來。
已回到原本巨大身材的巨人很自豪地走向提姆，並給他一個巨大的擁抱！

提姆 ▸ （抬頭跟巨人說話）你又再度成為真正的巨人了！

巨人 ▸ （很高興）是的，現在每次你激怒我時，可要小心了！

提姆 ▸ 可不是開玩笑的！真替你感到開心！你終於可以爬上豌豆回家了！

巨人 ▸ 謝啦！我的確想我老婆了。

提姆 ▸ （用手肘輕碰巨人一下）小別勝新婚，是不是啊，大個兒？

時尚王 ▸ 今晚實在太值得慶祝了！（他舉起酒杯敬酒）敬提姆和他的勇氣！

每個人 ▸ 敬提姆和他的勇氣！

提姆 ▸ 謝謝你們，喔，我們應該來個快樂結局大合照。（他拿出自拍神器，並請所有人圍繞在他身邊）等我將照片放上去 Instagram 之後，會通知你們的。

| 時尚王 | 提姆，你回家之後，代我向巫師問好，也讓他知道這裡隨時都歡迎他回來。 |

| 提姆 | 好，就這麼辦。 |

Phrases & Sentence Patterns慣用語 & 句型

❶ drive someone nuts 發瘋；抓狂（= drive someone crazy）

❷ out of one's hands 束手無策；不再由…掌管

❸ a sight for sore eyes 樂於看到的人或事；極有吸引力的人或事

❹ work up something 激發，激起

❺ be bummed out 感到憂鬱；感到難過

❻ Good/best things come in small packages.（強調）好東西未必總是大大的（這句有時候也拿來安慰身材矮小的人，強調個頭嬌小不見得是壞事）

❼ get a rise out of someone 激怒某人

❽ Absence makes the heart grow fonder. 小別勝新婚

Cultural Note

One time I traveled to New York to visit a friend. I took a taxi from the airport to my friend's place. After the taxi driver helped me unload the luggage from the trunk, I thanked him and happily dragged my luggage to my friend's apartment. Once the taxi driver was gone, I suddenly remembered that I forgot to tip him! No wonder I noticed a slightly awkward facial expression from the taxi driver' after he unloaded my luggage. Giving a tip is a norm in the United States whenever people provide you with a service, such as ordering a pizza delivered to your place, getting your haircut in a salon, or going to a spa. When you dine in a restaurant, tips are also expected. The range of the tip varies, depending on the service/ products. Typically, it ranges from 10 percent to 20 percent of the before-tax price. Therefore, the price you pay will be the after-tax price plus the tips you give.

文化角落

有一次筆者到紐約找朋友玩，下了機場之後直接搭計程車到朋友家樓下。計程車司機幫我從後車廂拿出行李之後，我跟他道謝並很開心地拖著行李往朋友的公寓走去。計程車開走時，我才忽然想起來自己忘了給他小費！難怪我當時注意到，當他幫我將行李拿出來時，臉上有一點奇怪的神情。給小費在美國是常態，只要別人為你提供服務，像是外送披薩到你家門口，去美髮店剪頭髮，或是去做全身按摩。當你在餐廳用餐時，也要給小費。小費的範圍則因不同服務有差。一般來說，會落在稅前總消費額的百分之十到二十之間。因此，你所消費的總額即是稅後總消費額加上你所給的小費。

During the celebration, Snow White takes Prince Charming to meet the Queen.

Snow White — Mother, I would like you to meet Prince Charming.

Prince Charming — (*bowing*) Your Majesty.

The Queen — Nice to meet you again, Prince Charming.

Snow White — (*talking to Prince Charming*) Will you excuse us for a second?

While Snow White drags the Queen aside to talk in private, Prince Charming walks over to Tim to ask for a favor.

Snow White — You know him?

The Queen — Of course! He was the one I tried to set you up with on a blind date, but you had to run away!

Snow White — Really? Oh, we're meant to be!

The Queen — I feel relieved. Finally, I don't need to trick you into eating my apple.

Snow White — Your apple? You were the Peasant Wife?

The Queen — Yes. The special potion in the apple was supposed to help you change your perspectives about men.

Snow White — I thought I had pretty good taste.

The Queen — That's not what you said to me when you fell out of love.

Snow White — You know I was just venting.

The Queen — I really just want you to find someone who will see you as the most precious apple in his eye.

Snow White — (hugging the Queen) Awww... I love you!

After figuring out what Prince Charming wants, Tim combines several

songs together in his music mixer app and connects his laptop to some portable speakers. Soon, the melody is filling the air. Then Prince Charming gets down on one knee and looks into Snow White's eyes with keen affection.

Prince Charming — Snow White... Will you marry me?

Snow White — Oh! Yes, of course!

The Queen — Not so fast, young lady! Although he was the one I wanted to set you up with, you shouldn't say 'yes' right away to someone you just met for the very first time.

Snow White — Oh my... you're right Mama. I'm sorry, Prince Charming.

The Queen — That's my girl. (*She turns to Prince Charming.*) I'm going to keep my eye on you for one year before I can allow you to officially ask for her hand.

Prince Charming — (*sighing*) Yes, Your Majesty.

Tim — (*patting Prince Charming's back*) It'll be alright

buddy. Trust me, she's a better queen than the one I read about.

　　在慶祝的時候，白雪公主帶白馬王子去見皇后。

白雪公主 ▸ 母后，我想要讓你見見白馬王子。

白馬王子 ▸ （鞠躬）皇后陛下您好。

皇后 ▸ 很高興再次見到你，白馬王子。

白雪公主 ▸ （跟白馬王子說）可以讓我們單獨講一下話嗎？
當白雪公主將皇后拉到旁邊私下談話時，白馬王子走到提姆那邊，請他幫個忙。

白雪公主 ▸ 您認識他？

皇后 ▸ 當然！他就是那位我試著幫你安排的相親對象，可是你一直跑掉！

白雪公主 ▸ 真的嗎？喔，我們真的註定在一起！

皇后 ▸ 真的鬆一口氣了，終於不用再騙你吃我的蘋果了。

白雪公主 ▸ 您的蘋果？您就是那村婦？

皇后 ▸ 是的，那蘋果裡有特別的配方，本來是要幫助你改變對男人的看法。

白雪公主　我以為我看男人的眼光還挺好的。

皇后　你失戀時可不是這麼對我說的。

白雪公主　您明知我只是在發洩。

皇后　我真的只是希望，你可以找到一個人，將你視為他眼中最珍貴的寶貝。

白雪公主　（擁抱皇后）喔…我愛你！
在了解白馬王子的請求之後，提姆用一個混音應用程式將一些音樂結合在一起，然後將他的筆記型電腦連接在幾個攜帶型擴音器上面。很快地，空氣中瀰漫著好聽的旋律。接著，白馬王子單膝下跪，並帶著熱切愛慕之意的眼神，注視著白雪公主。

白馬王子　白雪公主…嫁給我吧？

白雪公主　喔！我願意！

皇后　這位小姐，別這麼急！雖然他是我要你相親的對象，你也不應該立刻答應一個初次見面的人的求婚。

白雪公主　喔，母后，您說得對。白馬王子，真的很抱歉。

皇后　這樣才是我的乖女兒！（她轉向白馬王子）在我答應將她交到你手上之前，我會好好地觀察你一年的。

白馬王子　（歎一口氣）是的，皇后陛下。

提姆　　（拍拍白馬王子的背）兄弟，不要緊的，相信我，皇后比我所知道的版本還要好了。

Phrases & Sentence Patterns慣用語 & 句型

❶ in private 私下

❷ a blind date 相親

❸ meant to be 注定好的

❹ fall out of love 失戀

❺ apple in one's eye 珍貴的人或事物

❻ That's my girl.（通常用來讚美女孩或母的動物）乖女孩；乖孩子

❼ keep an eye on something or someone 注意；留意

❽ ask for her hand（用在詢問女方父母）徵求同意結婚

Cultural Note

In Taiwan, when a couple decides to get married, the tradition is that the groom and/or his family will be responsible for the wedding, whereas the bride's family will prepare the dowry. There are also traditional engagement ceremonies and an engagement reception. In the U.S., after a man proposes to a woman, they are engaged. There is typically no official ceremony or reception for the couple's engagement. The couple will start preparing for their wedding reception, which the bride and her family are generally responsible for most of the costs. However, it does not mean that the groom does not feel any pressure before his proposal. The nerve-racking "meeting the parents" scenario is common before he asks his girlfriend's father/mother for permission to marry their daughter. Another difference is that it is not common to take pre-wedding photos. Instead, most couples will hire a photographer for the day of their wedding when they both look pretty and handsome!

文化角落

　　在台灣，一對佳偶決定要結婚時，傳統上是新郎以及（或是）他的家人要負擔婚禮費用，而新娘的家人準備嫁妝，也會有傳統的訂婚儀式和訂婚宴客。在美國，男生和女生求婚之後即是訂婚了，一般來說沒有正式的訂婚儀式或宴客。然後新人就會開始籌備他們的婚禮宴客，通常是女方和她的家人負擔大部份的費用。不過，這不代表準新郎在求婚前就不會感受到任何壓力。在獲得女朋友的父親／母親的同意，將他們的女兒交給他之前，令人神經緊繃的「拜見女方父母」的場面也很常見。另一個不同於台灣的地方是，美國婚禮不拍宴客前的婚紗照，而是會在婚禮那天請一位攝影師，為他們捕捉當天最美最帥的樣子。

 MP3 46

While Prince Charming is dancing with Snow White, the Queen is chatting with Tim.

Tim How's your online dating going?

The Queen We've been going steady for a while now... virtually.

Tim Well, I think the guy you're dating online is the Wizard!

The Queen What? No way! That could be a deal breaker!

Tim Why? I would think he's a great catch!

The Queen (*showing him the Wizard's profile photo*) This is MY boyfriend. I don't remember the Wizard being this young and attractive.

Tim (*chuckling*) I think that's a photo of some famous football player. But look at your own

profile photo! You've uploaded Taylor Swift's photo!

The Queen ► Yeah... I guess it is an idealized image. But once my boyfriend sees my true colors, he will forgive me and love me for my inner beauty!

Tim ► That's why you need to meet him! He might be a good match for you. Come home with me and swing by his place to surprise him!

The Queen ► No no no! That's not gonna work!

Tim ► You'll never know unless you try!

The Queen ► Okay... I guess it won't hurt to give it a go.

After the party, Tim travels back to Chicago with the Queen, the new Mouse King and the Wolf. While the Queen goes straight to surprise the Wizard at his mansion, the new Mouse King and the Wolf are having a good time watching a movie with Tim's family. Later, when Tim is finally lying down in his cozy bed, his mother knocks on the door to tell Tim there's somebody here to see him. He goes downstairs and sees Prince Charming standing by the fireplace, who is very distressed and restless.

Tim ▸ What's wrong?

Prince Charming ▸ Snow White has been kidnapped!

Tim ▸ What!

Prince Charming ▸ While we were taking a walk in the field, a big airship came out of the sky and took her away. Then I found this note.

An eye for an eye.
Farewell!
The happily-ever-after ending.
R.

Tim ▸ Who's R?

Prince Charming ▸ I have no idea.

Tim ▸ Maybe The Queen knows...

Tim texts the Wizard to give him a heads-up:
Sorry to ruin your night with the Queen.
But I must tell you!!!
Snow White has been kidnapped!

Prince Charming and I are on our way to your place!
To be continued.

第五場

當白馬王子和白雪公主跳舞的時候，皇后正在和提姆聊天。

提姆 ▶ 你的線上約會進行的如何呢？

皇后 ▶ 目前穩定交往了好一陣子了…虛擬世界中。

提姆 ▶ 我覺得您正在約會的對象是巫師！

皇后 ▶ 什麼？不可能！這可是會造成分手的主因！

提姆 ▶ 為什麼！？我覺得他是個好對象！

皇后 ▶ （給他看巫師的大頭照）這才是我的男朋友，我不記得巫師的樣子有這麼年輕吸引人。

提姆 ▶ （呵呵笑）我想這是某個有名橄欖球員的照片，不過看一下您自己的大頭照！上傳的是泰勒·泰勒絲（Ｔaylor Swift）的照片耶！

皇后 ▶ 恩…那是我想要的理想形象。不過一旦我男朋友真的懂我了，他會原諒我，並且愛我的內在美的！

提姆 ▶ 所以才說您必須和他見面！他可能很適合您，和我一起回家，然後順便去他家給他一個驚喜！

皇后　　不不不！這行不通的！

提姆　　除非您試看看，不然永遠不會知道行不行得通的！

皇后　　好吧…我想試一下也無傷大雅。
派對之後，提姆和皇后，新鼠王以及野狼回到芝加哥。皇后直接去巫師的莊園給他一個驚喜。新鼠王和野狼則和提姆的家人一起看電影，度過愉快的時光。之後，當提姆終於可以躺在他那舒適的床上時，他媽媽敲他的房門，說有人來找他。他一下樓就看到白馬王子站在壁爐旁，看起來非常苦惱不安。

提姆　　怎麼了？

白馬王子　白雪公主被綁架了！

提姆　　什麼！？

白馬王子　當我們在田野裡散步時，一艘很大的飛船從天而降並帶走了她，然後我發現這張紙條。

以牙還牙，
再會了！！
那從此過著幸福快樂的日子。
R.

提姆　　誰是 R？

白馬王子　我不知道。

提姆傳簡訊給巫師，先簡單說明了一下。

很抱歉破壞了你和皇后的夜晚

可是我必須跟你說！！！

白雪公主被綁架了！

白馬王子和我正在去你家的路上！

待續。

Phrases & Sentence Patterns慣用語 & 句型

❶ go steady 穩定交往

❷ a deal breaker 某個問題或事情成為一個協議談不成的或一段關係分手的重要因素

❸ a great catch 不可失的好對象

❹ true colors （一個人的）本性

❺ a good match 倆人是適合的對象；匹配

❻ swing by one's place 順道拜訪（= stop by）

❼ an eye for an eye 以眼還眼

❽ give someone a heads-up 事先提醒要發生的某事

Cultural Note

Attending social events is usually one of the common ways people meet their Mr./Mrs. Right. Some people are even lucky enough to marry their high school sweetheart! However, that's not always possible, especially when you live in a very small town with few social events or limited dating prospects for you to choose from. To improve the odds of finding their life partner, people can start online dating as well. It is common to see TV commercials for popular online dating companies promoting their product. For online dating tips, the Internet is definitely a resourceful place to look! For entertainment related to dating, there's a popular reality show on TV called The Bachelor and it's sister show The Bachelorette. The premise of the show follows a single man, or woman, who's presented with 25 potential mates to choose as his/her life partner. Without surprise, all the participants are extremely attractive. This may not be a very realistic dating scenario for people trying to find their life partner, but this kind of show is definitely a pleasure to watch!

　　遇見自己的白馬王子或白雪公主的常用管道是透過參加社交活動。有些人很幸運,甚至可以在高中就遇見真愛!可是要在高中就碰到真愛很難,尤其當你是住在非常小的城鎮,社交活動幾乎少得可憐或僅有一些人選供選擇時。為了增加找到人生伴侶的機率,人們開始了線上交友,在美國常會看到一些有名的線上交友公司買電視廣告,推銷公司的服務。有關線上交友的訣竅,網路絕對是一個很好的資源!和約會有關的休閒娛樂當中,電視真人秀的「單身漢」和與之相呼應的「單身女郎」很受歡迎,這節目的前提是,一個單身漢或單身女郎要從25位候選人當中選出自己的人生伴侶。毫無疑問地,所有的參選者都非常地美麗帥氣,這樣的節目或許不是一般人尋找人生伴侶的真實約會情境,但無疑地讓人看起來非常賞心悅目。

Learn Smart! 052

童話奇緣 Follow Kuso 英語童話，來一場穿越時空之旅 (MP3)

作　　者　克莉斯汀・愛佐
封面構成　高鍾琪
內頁構成　菩薩蠻數位文化有限公司

發 行 人　周瑞德
執行總監　齊心瑀
企劃編輯　陳韋佑
執行編輯　饒美君
校　　對　陳欣慧、魏于婷
印　　製　大亞彩色印刷製版股份有限公司
初　　版　2015 年 11 月
定　　價　新台幣 380 元
出　　版　倍斯特出版事業有限公司
電　　話　(02) 2351-2007
傳　　真　(02) 2351-0887
地　　址　100 台北市中正區福州街 1 號 10 樓之 2
E - m a i l　best.books.service@gmail.com
網　　址　www.bestbookstw.com

港澳地區總經銷　泛華發行代理有限公司
地　　　　址　香港新界將軍澳工業邨駿昌街 7 號 2 樓
電　　　　話　(852) 2798-2323
傳　　　　真　(852) 2796-5471

國家圖書館出版品預行編目(CIP)資料

童話奇緣：Follow Kuso 英語童話,來一場穿越
時空之旅 / 克莉斯汀.愛佐著.-- 初版.-- 臺
北市：倍斯特, 2015.11 面；　公分.--
(Learn smart! ; 52)
ISBN 978-986-91915-5-5 (平裝附光碟片)
1.英語 2.讀本
　　　805.18　104021549